WALLABY MY LOVE

AN M/M SHIFTER MPREG ROMANCE

RIVER'S EDGE
BOOK 8

LORELEI M. HART

ARIA GRACE

SURRENDERED PRESS

CONTENTS

PROLOGUE
WALLY

"Go!" Sean held open the door to my cell and waved me through. "Hurry. They're coming."

Adrenaline flowed through my veins as I rushed to his side. He'd been paid to guard me for the terrible people who ran The Lab, but Sean was different. He wasn't a monster like the others. He promised to save me. Save us all. "Where are we going?"

"You're getting the hell out of here." His arm was stiff as he pointed his gun down the corridor. "Head to the south exit. The door is unlocked. Wait for me there. I'll get there as soon as I get everyone else out."

"No." I couldn't leave without him. "I'll wait. Tell me what to do."

He shook his head and grabbed my arm, tugging me along. "You need to get out. I'll just be a few minutes."

"I can help." I tripped over my feet and almost landed on my face.

"Dammit, Wally." He held me against his side, almost carrying me as he ran toward the unlocked door. "You're gonna get us both killed. Just wait for me outside. I'll be quick."

I didn't want to leave him, but I was wasting time by arguing. The faster I let him get to the other cells, the sooner he and I could be together. Forever. At least, that was what I told myself as I took a deep breath and then ran through the door.

There were alarms and flashing lights and the occasional boom that sounded like gunfire but could have been anything. I'd gotten used to hearing the occasional lab explosion during my time there. How long had it been? Two years? Three? It was hard to keep track after so long.

But I was finally free. As I approached the fence, I realized I needed to shift. It had been a long time since I had the freedom to shift at will, but the instinct was still there. Just as a spotlight landed on the lawn ten yards in front of me, my body shifted into its fur and the wallaby that lived within me took control. He moved with more grace and power than I ever could, so I retreated into my mind, allowing my animal to keep me alive.

All I had to do was stay alive.

Sean was counting on me to get free of the fence line and past the river. As long as I made it that far, I'd be fine. And very soon, he'd be with me again. My human thoughts drifted into the background as the sounds around me got louder and more frantic.

I could just barely register that we were in water when the loudest boom I'd ever heard in my life reverberated through us. It was too late to turn back and look, but I knew what had happened. The Lab had exploded… and Sean was still in it. Probably. Maybe.

But he promised to meet me. He promised he was just behind me. All I had to do was be patient and he'd come get me. He'd save me again. Just like he promised.

My head was foggy, so I didn't put too much effort into concentrating. When I focused through the eyes of my wallaby, all I could see was darkness. And when I scented the air, only a heavy cloud of smoke filled my nostrils.

Sean wasn't back yet. But he would be.

I retreated into my mind, relinquishing control to my wallaby once more. I didn't need to be present until Sean arrived. When he found me, crouching in whatever hole we were tucked into, I'd come back to myself. I'd become the man he cared about and we could live happily ever after.

Soon.

But when was *soon*?

My eyes opened up every now and then, but my head still felt cloudy, so the minutes felt like days. Or maybe the days felt like minutes. It wasn't clear but there was sunlight, so maybe it was morning. Or afternoon. I closed my eyes against the bright light and retreated once again.

Sean wasn't back yet. Maybe he was helping others. That was the kind of man he was. And when he was done with them, he'd find me. Soon.

My wallaby was drinking from the river and it was dark outside. Was it nighttime already? How much time had passed? Twelve hours? Maybe twenty-four? Longer? It couldn't be longer. But when I thought back to how many times it had gone from light to dark, it seemed possible that many days had passed.

And Sean hadn't returned for me. Did he forget about me? Did he think I had left him, so he'd kept running? That wasn't possible. He knew I'd never leave without him. And in my heart, I knew he wouldn't leave without me.

Which left only one other scenario.

The scenario I wasn't ready to face yet.

The scenario that made my head pound even harder.

So I let the terrible thought float out of my consciousness as I went back to sleep.

Again.

When I was asleep, I didn't feel alone. It wasn't clear who was with me, but there were others. Others from The Lab. People and animals like me who were just as scared as I was. And a few who were happy. Those were the connections I held on to the tightest. When my head was clear, I was able to almost feel what they were feeling. See what they were seeing. Communicate with them in a way that only a shifter could.

So I drifted out of reality and settled into my new happy place. The place in my head where others were safe and happy…and Sean was still looking for me. The place where I could pretend he was checking every den, bush, and shed for miles…and he wouldn't give up until he found me.

And I wouldn't give up on him.

I couldn't give up on him.

He was the only person in my life who cared about me more than anyone else. Even my parents were more interested in the bounty they received from The Lab than about keeping me safe.

ONE
SEAN

He got away.

He got away.

He got away.

Regardless of what happened to me, knowing Wally was safe and free was all that mattered. Repeating those words in my head was the only thing that kept me going when they were beating me for almost twelve hours after the initial escape. And it was what continued to keep me alive when I was being transported to a different lab—but not as a guard this time.

I was put in a cell and marked for experimentation. Just like all the omegas I'd been charged with supervising for the past year.

But I wasn't like all the omegas. As a stallion alpha, I couldn't breed whatever the hell they were trying to breed. Which meant they had to come up with something different for me.

Something worse.

Much, much worse.

It had been at least several days since the escape. Maybe longer. I really didn't know. Being locked in a dark cage made it hard to tell time, and meal times weren't exactly consistent. At least, it didn't feel like they were. Maybe the trays of moldy bread and other unidentifiable proteins were arriving on an eight-hour interval. But based on the extreme hunger that consumed my entire body, I thought it was more like a forty-eight or seventy-two-hour interval.

And I'd only received a few trays.

Which meant it might have only been a week. And more importantly, Wally was far away from those monsters. The monsters who bought him like cattle and used him in ways that I couldn't even imagine.

I thought I was there to help society. To advance science. At least, that was what they told me. And I was stupid enough to believe them. When I was hired for three times the going salary, I should have known something was wrong. But I pretended I was worth all that money. That my references had said such amazing things about me to warrant a premium wage.

But none of that was true.

I wasn't there to make the world a better place. I wasn't there to protect the innocent by guarding the enemy. I was hired to ensure innocent omegas were enslaved by evil men who called themselves doctors so they could benefit from the lives and deaths of those omegas.

I was a fool.

But not anymore.

Once I realized what was happening, I couldn't just look the other way. Especially not after getting to know Wally. He was so kind and gentle, always taking care of the other omegas, even when he was at his weakest. Which was why I had to get him—and everyone else— out of there.

And I did. It wasn't easy, but we did it.

Wally and I spent weeks planning exactly how it would go and where we would meet up after everyone was out. Everything went smoothly…until it didn't. And I hated that I wasn't able to fulfill my promise to meet up with him.

But I was captured and transported before there was any chance of getting a message to him. I would think about him every day of my life, but I hoped more than anything that he had already forgotten about me. He probably waited around a few hours and then took off for greener pastures.

At least, that was what I'd hoped had happened.

I hoped he'd forgotten all about me because he was in a cute little town with lots of friends and lots of space to hop around and have a happy life.

My days might have been numbered, and I hoped they were, because whatever was in store for me wouldn't be pleasant, but I was comforted by the fact that Wally was finally happy. He could enjoy his life and find someone to love.

Even if that someone wasn't me.

But that was no longer an option.

The echoing sound of heavy footfalls pulled me out of my thoughts and set me on edge. They were coming back. The guards who held the job I used to hold. I tried to talk sense into them, explaining that what they were doing was wrong and they were helping monsters hurt, and in most cases, kill innocent omegas. But they didn't believe me or didn't care. One guy punched me in the side of the head and stuck a needle in my neck.

That was when I realized I would die there.

"Hey, you, wake up!" A metal tray tapped the bars of my enclosure. It was dark, but I could make out the shapes of two well-muscled alphas.

If I were properly fed and hydrated, I would have tried to take them out and make a run for it. But in my weakened state, I could hardly get in a few push-ups before needing a break, so I just stayed in the corner, out of their way. "I'm up."

"Chow time!" The lock on the door clicked open and the door swung toward me.

I didn't move an inch. I'd learned early on that even the slightest movement was taken as a threat. They also expected gratitude for their torture. "Thanks."

Nothing on the tray was appealing, but I was too hungry to be picky. I waited just long enough for them to leave before devouring the scraps they offered. And as soon as I had some calories in me, I closed my eyes again and thought about Wally.

This time, my mind didn't dwell on the past or the future that would never be. I dreamt about the present, but it was more of a nightmare. Wally wasn't happily enjoying life. He was scared and alone…and silent. And as hard as I tried to wake up from that terrible reality, I couldn't do it.

It felt real and present, and…it broke my heart.

TWO
WALLY
(TWO WEEKS LATER)

I was grateful for being found. Really I was. Being taken someplace safe meant more to me than they could know…especially given that I still hadn't spoken a single word to anyone.

So much of it was a blur. I still didn't completely understand how Ward, Goodman, and Holden were all able to sense me, but somehow they did, and they took me away. Away from the burned rubble of The Lab and away from the nightmare that was once my life, but also away from Sean.

He wouldn't know where to find me. Sean promised to come back for me, and when he did, I'd be gone.

The whole situation was confusing in my disoriented state. I wasn't even sure exactly where I was geographically or even what time of year it was. And since I still couldn't shift back to my skin, I had to either suck it up and be grateful or suck it up and be miserable. I tried to go for option A, but it wasn't easy. I decided to just accept at face value that I was safe in the little farmhouse. I'd take my skin again one day. Probably not today, but eventually.

Fortunately, I didn't hate it there. Not really. I'd lived in far worse circumstances.

The Lab was the worst, for sure.

Not hating the farm and the people who gave me food and shelter was not the same thing as thriving. I was going through the motions of life without actually living it. And being stuck in my wallaby form didn't help matters at all. I wanted to talk to the people who were kind enough to rescue me and tell them who I was and why I needed to go back and find Sean. Instead, the best I could do to communicate was eat the foods that I loved with abandon so they knew I preferred them. And we'd figured out how to indicate yes and no, but that was about it. Not what I'd call the best kind of communication, but it would have to do for now.

And it wasn't that I didn't try to shift, or that I'd given up hope. Shifting was my main focus each and every day. I would try and try and try again. Failing each time in a fit of frustration and humiliation. And I wasn't alone in my attempts.

Auggie tried to help me shift. *Fail.*

Jase tried to help me shift. *Nothing.*

Doc tried to help me shift. *Not even one hair left my body.*

The end result each time was that they felt like they had somehow failed me, and I wanted to give up and not risk that failure again. Of course, it wasn't their fault I was trapped inside my beast. If they could change it so I wasn't, they would have in a heartbeat.

They were good people.

It was The Lab's fault. I hated that place and all the people involved in it with every fiber of my being. The "doctors" and "lab techs" were made of pure evil. They got off on trying to mutate and manipulate my DNA to make some kind of a super shifter and why? For profit and power, of course.

Rumors at The Lab were they thought they'd accomplished it. I called bullshit on that. If they had, it wouldn't have just been rumors. They would have doubled down on all of us, attempting to recreate whatever they had done.

But I got out before I knew for sure what was true or not. And now that I was gone, I needed to stop reliving the horrors from that period of my life. It was time to move forward. I couldn't change a single thing that happened to me at The Lab, but I could take away their power to make me miserable and I planned to do exactly that.

Needing a distraction, I hopped into the barn to visit my friend Daisy. Technically, she was a pig, but in many ways, she acted more like a dog. And for whatever reason, she took a liking to my wallaby from the second we arrived. That was why we'd often go on adventures together. How that must've looked to the humans.

Adventures akin to wandering around the farm and seeking out treats, usually. Maybe it wasn't everyone's definition of an adventure, but after being in a cage for so long, any kind of wandering outdoors was exciting.

And it was nice to not be alone.

When I looked around, Daisy wasn't snoozing in the shade, which was where I'd last seen her. So much for going on a walk with her today. That meant I had to wander on my own, which was fine. Really, it was. It wasn't as if Daisy was a human companion. I hadn't had one of those in a long time. Far too long.

"Wally!" Auggie called me from the house. "Wally!"

I hopped out of the barn and looked around until I saw him on the front porch. In his hand was a basket.

"There you are. Xander brought you a treat." Xander was Doc's kid, although not really a kid anymore. He came around from time to time to hang with Auggie and Jase. And just like all the other people I'd met in River's Edge, he was extremely nice to me.

And today, he'd brought me something to eat. I wasn't that picky about my food. Not at all. But being human, Auggie was sure I needed variety, and that train of thought had probably rubbed off on Xander.

As soon as I reached him, he lowered the basket. "Have you ever had fiddleheads?"

We'd sort of worked out our own style of communication. I raised one arm for yes and two for no. So far, it had worked out pretty well.

You know what would work out better? If you let me have my skin back.

And just like every time I complained to my wallaby about this, he ignored me.

I raised both arms to let Auggie know I had no idea what those were in his basket. They looked good, though, and I was willing to give them a try.

He set the basket down so I could see inside. "You're in for a treat. I love them. Of course, I saute them with olive oil and garlic, and you'll be dining on them raw, but still…so delicious."

Upon closer inspection, they looked like baby ferns. I liked ferns well enough and grabbed one to try. He was right. They were delicious. I took back everything I ever thought about not wanting variety in my diet. If there were more things out there as tasty as these, I wanted them all.

"I also bought you something." He gestured toward the far side of the porch. "And before you get upset that I got you a dog bed—it isn't. It's designed for humans, and I thought you might like it."

I hopped to him and rubbed my head against his side. Even if it was a dog bed, I'd have appreciated the gesture. I had a pig for a best friend. I wasn't a species-ist.

"You're welcome." He squatted down until he was eye level with me. "I know it must suck being trapped in there. But I promise you, if there's a way to get you unstuck, Doc will find it."

I believed him.

Doc was a good man. He didn't just test on me, instead asking for my consent each step of the way. Informed consent, at that. I always knew everything he intended to do and why, long before he actually started it. At first, I thought it odd that so much time at The Lab had trained me to think torture was normal. I hated it. But now, I appreciated the kindness he offered me for what it was.

I went back to eating the fiddleheads, and Auggie went inside, telling me to just push the door open and come on in if I needed anything. He was sure to remind me of that often. I never did and probably never would. But taking a nap on my new bed? That was something I was definitely going to do.

Belly full, I settled into the soft pillow and closed my eyes, slumber coming quickly.

In my dreams, I was always human. Always. And today's dream was no exception. Only thing was, I might as well have been a wallaby because I was unable to speak or write in my dreams. I just wandered around until I found a stallion—my stallion.

I didn't know how I knew he was mine, but he was. He was my stallion, and I was his wallaby. That's just how it was…how it was meant to be.

I walked over to him, his stall dark—so dark. The stench around us was worse than a barn that hadn't been mucked out yet. It was filth and shit, as well as an overpowering chemical stench.

There was so much I wanted to say to him, but words weren't possible. Instead, I petted his nose the way he liked until I felt him getting dragged farther and farther away as someone ripped him out of reach.

I opened my mouth to scream—not a sound came out.

My head popped up, my body torn from my sleep by a hissing sound. Not just any hissing either, it was me. My beast was hissing the sound that the dream me couldn't make. Maybe I needed to stop with the afternoon naps.

No part of me was refreshed after a dream like that.

As the days dragged on, it was getting harder and harder to distinguish the real world from fantasy.

In reality, I was slowly starving to death in a cell and being pumped full of drugs while they did things to me that I was thankfully not conscious enough to understand. But when I allowed my fantasies to take over, I was floating on a cloud and talking to Wally again. He was strong and healthy, calling me to him. He was safe, so that made me happy. But knowing that he was still waiting for me to go to him left me with a longing inside that felt so real.

Not just "vivid dream" kind of real…but I could almost feel him. Like that was a real calling from Wally that I needed to listen to. And I tried, I really did, but it was all in vain. He would be gone and I was back here… back at The Lab.

As I had for the thousandth time, I called to my inner stallion and tried to pull him forward. But with the drugs and the hunger, my body wasn't in any kind of shape to shift. I just needed to wait a little longer until I could somehow manage to build back some strength. If only it were that easy.

Nothing about this was easy.

At this rate, I'd either die from hunger or I'd die trying to escape. And escape wasn't looking like a viable option. Which pretty much meant I was going to die… and that sucked.

There was no good outcome for me, but I'd made my choices, and I didn't regret them. Given the chance to save Wally again, I'd do it over and over. Getting through this last stage was easier now that I could feel Wally's presence. It was an indescribable sensation of him being in and around me…even though I knew he was miles away. Hopefully, hundreds or thousands of miles away. Far enough that he would never be found by the evil zealots who ran The Lab.

I closed my eyes and tried to conjure up an image of him. His green eyes sparkling with hope and emotion on the day he escaped. The way he held his hand out to me as he backed away, willing me to grab it and go with him, even though he knew I had more work to do. We'd discussed it extensively and both knew he would get out first…and I would follow behind once everyone else was freed.

I promised I'd be there.

A promise I didn't keep…a promise I couldn't keep.

Before I could spiral too far into my self-loathing and despair, the familiar footsteps of a lab guard echoed in the chamber. I kept my eyes closed for as long as possible, even after my arm was yanked forward. I stumbled to my feet and was dragged down the hallway to an experimentation room…again.

Fortunately, the needle went into my neck almost as soon as my ass hit the chair. The drugs kept me from retaining any memories of what they were doing to me. I didn't want to know. I never wanted to know, especially after I became conscious and I saw the aftermath of what they'd done. This time, when I woke up in my cell, there were ragged cuts and dried blood all over my body.

But they didn't matter.

I was getting closer to the end. I could feel it. I was waiting for it.

The unexpected pull of my stallion startled me. It had been so long since I'd felt him in me that I was surprised by his presence. There was no way to shift in the small cell. He'd never fit. But the nagging urge to come forward was unlike anything I'd felt before.

From the time of my first shift, I'd always been in full control.

Whenever I wanted to shift, I called upon my stallion and relinquished control of my body. Never before had he tried to force his way into being. I felt bad for the animal that was probably feeling even more oppressed by the small space than I was in my human form.

Animals were not meant to be in cages. And being contained for too long would break them, and that's what I feared had happened to my stallion. But here he was being pushier than ever. My whole body shook as he tried to emerge, blurring the edges around my human form.

What the hell?

For the first time, I noticed that the door to my cell was not fully closed. The alignment was off by just a centimeter, but if the latch wasn't completely engaged, I knew I might be able to open the door. I tried not to get my hopes up as I crawled as silently as I could to the door and gave it a push.

My heart started pounding in my chest as metal scraped against metal and the door slowly swung open. There was enough noise from the squeaky door that I was sure a guard would be running down the hall at any second. Every little sound echoed through those halls.

Which meant I had less than a second to react.

I somehow managed to get up and then I took off at full speed, allowing a wave of adrenaline to power my legs directly toward the exit. The door was locked, but that didn't slow me down. I pulled back and relinquished control of my body to my stallion then let him do what was needed. My shift was short, and I was instantly standing on all fours.

He took a few steps back and then reared up on his hind legs, walking forward and dropping all his massive weight on the wooden door. It cracked and splintered like a toothpick as we blasted through, taking off in the direction of the woods beyond the warehouse.

I tried to note landmarks as we ran through trees and brush, but we were moving too fast, and I was too weak. My stallion seemed to know where to go, so I was lulled nearly to sleep, not thinking about what would happen if we got caught. The pain and suffering would be over either way.

Now it was time to let fate decide my future.

The funny thing about fate was that it wasn't always what we anticipated.

Mostly, I was expecting a slow and painful death. Maybe being shot from behind as we ran away…or being captured with a net and tortured with even worse experiments than before. But nothing like that happened. We ran in the darkness, guided only by the light of the moon. I couldn't guess how long we galloped before I fell into a dream. And as soon as I did, Wally was there. His sparkling eyes were begging me to come to him, and I could almost feel a magnetic pull toward him.

The compulsion got stronger with every step we took, as if my stallion were reacting to that same magnet, allowing nature's tug to take us where we needed to be.

I held on to that image in my head for hours…maybe days. Time was a blur. I was in and out of consciousness. The only thing that existed was my stallion and I and our final destination, wherever that might be.

The sun rose and set a few times, with my beast stopping only long enough to drink from creeks or ponds before continuing forward. Not once did he allow himself to rest. He was on a mission.

And as I drifted off once again, I knew I would be with Wally soon. I didn't understand how I knew it, but I did. There was zero doubt in my mind. We would see him soon and fulfill our promise.

I didn't know what I would find when I got there, if he would even be alive or not, but I was on a path straight for him, and nothing would stop me this time.

Nothing.

FOUR

WALLY

Being an animal sucked. Okay, that wasn't true. I loved my wallaby, and I appreciated that he had kept me alive for so long after we escaped The Lab. But not having the power to shift back into my human form was definitely getting old, mostly because I couldn't communicate with anyone around me.

I wanted to stretch out my arms and take a hot shower and curl up in a bed wearing warm pajamas. They were silly things, but still, I longed for them. Being stuck in this form meant none of those things were going to happen anytime soon.

Jase and August had been wonderful to me, taking care of me as if I were a man, even though that meant sleeping on "not a" dog bed on their porch and eating a plant-based diet instead of the steaks I often saw them grilling in the yard.

But if I was being honest with myself, I was starting to get worried.

Would I ever be a man again?

Shifting was a natural part of my life, and suddenly losing the ability to change forms was scary. At first, it seemed like an instinctive reaction as a way for my body to protect me from the men of The Lab who might have been looking for me. And after I was rescued, I chalked it up to anxiety over being with strangers and the natural distrust I'd developed after being taken by the doctors.

But as time passed, it seemed less and less likely that I would ever be in my skin again. And that seriously hampered my companionship options, considering I was 10,000 miles away from any other wallaby mobs that I could potentially integrate with. It was increasingly looking like it would be Daisy and I against the world.

Resting my chin on my fist, I closed my eyes, letting the evening breeze wash over me as I thought about Sean. My thoughts were always on him, but in quiet moments, it was almost like I could feel him. Honestly,

I was probably losing touch with reality because now it was more than just a feeling. I could almost scent him in the air. I could have stayed in that moment forever but the sound of an animal approaching in the distance alerted me to a potential danger.

I snuck over to the corner of the porch, hiding behind August's rocking chair with my eyes trained on the woods. For the first time ever, I contemplated taking Auggie up on his offer to just push my way into the house. But if danger was running toward me, I owed it to them to not bring it into their home if I could. At least now if I was discovered, my hosts and their family would be safe or have a chance at safety.

The footsteps were heavy and loud, crashing through branches and debris, as if moving at a fast pace. August and Jase appeared on the porch, first glancing at me to make sure I was okay and then at the approaching visitor.

So much for me protecting them.

Jase put his arm around his mate and squinted into the dark. "Are we expecting anyone?"

"Not that I know of." August glanced toward me. "What about you? Any long-lost relatives we should know about?"

I wanted so badly to scream that there was nobody. I was alone in the world, and if somebody was coming for me, it was probably to kill me. But before I could attempt to shift yet again or even raise an arm, the silhouette of a huge horse appeared on the driveway.

It was Sean. My Sean. My stallion.

I'd never seen Sean's horse in person, but I knew it was him. His gaze locked on me as I jumped right off the porch and hopped toward him. As I approached, the animal disappeared and the man I'd been waiting so long for stood in front of me, arms open as I jumped up into them.

As a wallaby.

He held me against his chest and nuzzled my neck, not at all surprised that I wasn't human. "Wally, I've been so worried. I'm so glad you're okay."

Am I? Am I okay if I'm not a man? There were so many things I wanted to say to him, but I couldn't. Focusing all my energy on trying to shift didn't produce even a flutter. I felt nothing but the arms of the man who saved me, wrapped around my body after so much time apart.

Sean was there, and he was alive.

I'd been more and more worried that he lost his life saving mine and that my dreams were him coming from the beyond to let me know. But here, in his arms, I now knew that was not the case. He came back to me, just like he promised he would.

I sucked in a deep whiff of his scent, appreciating the unique aroma of his stallion mixed in the air. It was perfect. And real.

It is real, right?

I turned to look at August and Jase just to make sure I wasn't imagining all this.

They were smiling and didn't seem at all concerned by the naked man holding me, so I rubbed my chin against Sean's shoulder then took a little lick. It was wrong, for sure, but I couldn't resist. I'd wanted to do it for so long, and with so much bare skin available to me, it was the perfect time to do it.

A full-body shiver rocked through him as he sucked in a breath. "Why haven't you shifted?"

Jase stepped forward and cleared his throat. "Hi, there. I'm Jase, and this is my mate, August. I take it you know our wallaby friend?"

Sean's grip around me tightened slightly, and he nodded. "Yeah, hi. I'm Sean. I worked at The Lab and helped get Wally out."

I was afraid to look at their faces, knowing they would think badly of Sean once they realized he had been part of such an evil organization. How could they not? For all they knew, nothing good ever came from that place. But when I glanced between the two men who had taken me into their home, I was surprised to see nothing but curiosity.

No hostility at all.

"Then we owe you thanks," Auggie said with a smile. "When he was found, the building was nothing but a pile of charred bricks and metal, but no one knew how it happened, only that Wally needed a safe place to stay."

"By the time I knew what they were really doing, so much damage had been done." Guilt clung to Sean's voice, and I wanted to take it all away from him. Didn't he see that if it wasn't for him, I'd still be trapped there and tortured daily? That was if I was even still alive.

"If I could have gotten everybody out sooner, I would have." Sean dropped his chin to his chest. "I'm so sorry," he whispered into my ear, rubbing his cheek against mine. "So, so sorry."

"Let's get you both inside. We've been trying to get this one to shift since he arrived, but he either doesn't want to or isn't able to."

Instinctively, I nodded my head, looking right into Sean's eyes. I wanted him to know I wanted to shift. Desperately.

"But he's okay?" Sean's palm slid down the length of my body, feeling for injuries or damage. "Nothing's wrong with him?"

"Not that we can tell." Jase took a step back and waved toward the house. "Let's go inside and get you some clothes. We can have our friend Doc come by and check you out, if you'd like."

Again, I looked into Sean's eyes and nodded. It was also the first time I saw his body since he arrived. It was covered with scars and newly healed cuts. I looked away quickly, not wanting him to see my sadness over what he'd been through. He had enough to deal with without my grief and guilt piled on.

For the first time, he smiled. "Yeah, I think that would be okay."

FIVE
SEAN

Jase was about my size, so the sweats and shirt he handed me on the way to the shower fit fine. A little snug but better than walking around a stranger's house in my birthday suit. It felt beyond amazing being under the steamy water. I couldn't remember the last time I'd experienced such decadence. But the entire time I was in there, my mind kept wandering back to Wally.

Why hadn't he shifted yet? Had the things done to him at The Lab stolen his abilities? Had I saved him too late? Was he at least happy in his beast's form? His human side was in there for sure. He communicated in a way that left no room for doubt there. My fear was that he was in another prison; his own body.

I climbed out of the shower and reached for the towel, suddenly needing to get back to him, to show him that I was here and let him know I would do whatever it took to help him. My skin was still damp as I struggled to get my clothing on, and when I opened the bathroom door and walked out, I almost stepped on Wally, who was waiting for me right outside.

He was waiting for me. My Wally needed me near. Next time, I have to either take a speed shower or let him in. He'd waited for me long enough already.

Too long.

"Hey, there." I reached down, and he jumped right into my arms. He wasn't tiny, but there was no way I wouldn't hold him every time he needed me. "Sorry for taking so long. The hot water felt great on my joints."

Wally pressed all his weight against my chest, leaning into me with complete trust that I wouldn't let him fall.

Because I wouldn't. I was never letting him down again…ever.

"So, let's go see what this doctor guy has to say."

Auggie and Jase both agreed it was a good idea for Doc to look me over. And they were right. My body was a mess, not only visibly, but down deep. Not knowing what was done to me back at The Lab meant I had no clue how bad it was.

Wally stayed in my arms and we walked into the family room. There was an older man holding a black medical bag, an otter by the scent, waiting for us. August was playing with a baby on the floor, and Jase was doing something on his laptop. Had it not been for the medical bag, it would've looked like a quiet night of friends and family gathered for game night.

"Sean, this is Doc. He's our…doc." August stood up and placed the baby on his shoulder. "Doc, this is Sean. He helped Wally and others escape."

"It's a pleasure to meet you, Sean." The doctor gestured to a dining chair in the middle of the room, and I put Wally down. I hated to do it, but as long as he was in my arms, he wasn't free to move where he wanted to. And with a doctor nearby, I feared that might trigger a flight or fight response in him.

The "medical" community had not been kind to him— to either of us.

"Normally, I'd invite you to my office for an exam, but since it's late, and it doesn't seem like Wally is likely to let you out of his sight, we have you set up right here. If that's okay with you." There was a calmness to the man's voice, and I instantly trusted him.

"Sure." I indicated to Wally to have a seat on the sofa and took a seat across from him. I didn't know how much "humanness" his new friends allowed, but I refused to not at least offer him a comfortable seat.

"I appreciate your hospitality. I'm sorry for just showing up like this. I had no idea where we were heading until we got close enough that I could…" My words died on my tongue as I looked at Wally.

How could I explain what I felt? Nothing made sense. Not really.

"Could what, Sean?" Doc gently pointed a device into my ear and took a look. "What happened next?"

I trained my gaze on a knot in the hardwood floor and sighed. "I guess I could…sense he was here." After several long seconds, I took a peek around the room. "Is that weird?"

Doc smiled and shook his head just a bit. "Not at all. And we're glad you're here."

Wally bounced a little but didn't leave the couch.

"He seems pretty happy to see you too." Doc reached for his bag. "I'm not going to do anything invasive, but between your trip here and whatever caused the scars poking out from under your clothing, it's best that I at least take your vitals. And if you want everyone to leave, just let me know. Not one of them will mind… with one possible exception."

He meant Wally, and I had a feeling he was right. Wally wasn't ready to let me leave his side for long. Not yet, anyway.

While Doc poked at me, I thought about what they'd said earlier. I felt fine, so I wasn't worried about a thorough exam, but I think it made everyone else feel better to know I wasn't hiding anything. I appreciated how Doc explained his actions as he went and was beyond gentle.

It was quite a difference from my last experience.

After a few minutes, Doc took a step back and clasped his hands in front of his waist. "You look good—or at least like everything is healing nicely. If nothing's hurting or bothering you, I think we can consider you to be healthy as a horse." He smirked at his joke. "Do you have any questions for me?"

I shrugged. "Um, who are you guys? How do you all live together when you're all…different?" I turned to Wally and held out my arm.

He immediately jumped onto my lap and settled in. I instantly felt more at ease. It wasn't just Wally who needed me, apparently.

"And, uh, how did you find Wally?" They'd given me just enough information when I arrived to get me to agree to stay the night. Now, it was time for some real answers.

August walked back into the room with a plate of freshly baked cookies. I hadn't even noticed him leaving, my entire focus split between Wally and Doc. "That's a whole different story. You're gonna need a few of these."

I grabbed four and leaned back while they explained how they found Wally. I didn't realize how hungry I was until I took the first bite. They were amazing, as if baked up by some magic cookie fairy designed to lure you into their realm. And if that were the case, it would totally work.

I nearly choked on my bite when they mentioned fairies a few minutes into their explanation. Apparently, some of their friends were fae and had the ability to connect their minds with Wally's when he was waiting for me. They tracked him down and brought him back, but weren't able to help him shift. No one was sure why.

It could have been physical or emotional or mental… but regardless of the reason, there was no guarantee he'd ever be a man again.

"Before we get further…who made these cookies?" Now that I had that ridiculous notion in my head, it was starting to take root.

"I did." August puffed out his chest with pride. "Family recipe."

"They are amazing." I grabbed another one. "Do you think they're safe for Wally to eat?" Being a shifter was weird like that. As a human, we could eat all human foods, but in our animal forms, we had to follow the rules of our beast.

"Absolutely."

I immediately grabbed one for Wally, and he snatched it right up.

My arms automatically curled around him a little tighter, holding him close enough that I could feel the heat radiating off his body and his heart beating in time with mine as he nibbled away. He had quite the table manners for a wallaby, another indication that he was still very human in there.

"I'm just grateful that he's okay. Thank you for taking care of him." I looked each man in the eye, expressing my gratitude in the only way I could. "I don't know how to thank you properly, my words don't feel like even close to enough."

Doc stepped forward and placed a fatherly hand on my shoulder. "We should be thanking you for blowing up that wretched place. We have other friends who were victims of The Lab, so the fact that you were able to save so many people… Well, you're a hero as far as I'm concerned."

A lump formed in my throat, and I didn't know how to respond. "I'm no hero. I was stupid for a long time." I looked down at Wally in my arms and sighed. "And then I was selfish."

"We should let these two get some rest." Jase stood up and pulled August with him. "Help yourself to anything in the kitchen. We're up with the roosters but we'll leave breakfast on the stove for whenever you wake up. Sleep well!"

Before I could say anything else, they were walking Doc out the door, the child in their arms, and we were left alone. "Well, I guess it's bedtime."

He nodded and rested his head on my shoulder again.

This wasn't exactly what I had in mind when I thought about our first night together on the outside…but I would take Wally however I could have him. "Lead the way."

I put him down and followed him to the room we'd be staying in. There was one queen-sized bed in the middle of a cramped office/guest room/storage closet. Wally hopped up and went to the far side, sitting on the pillow as if waiting for me to make a move. Was he nervous that I wouldn't want to share a space with him as we slept, that I'd want his beast to sleep on the fancy dog bed his new friends had given him?

Unable to stifle a yawn, I stretched and then pulled back the comforter and sheet. I climbed inside, holding the sheet up high enough for Wally to scoot in beside me. Even though he wasn't the man I remembered him to be, it felt like he was there, far more present than I was when I shifted.

Like I was with Wally, the man.

The omega who stole my heart and changed me forever.

As soon as my eyes closed, and Wally was curled up at my side with his head on my shoulder, I drifted off. I was finally home. it might not be my house or my bed, but for me, home wasn't a place. It was a person. A being.

Wally was my home.

SIX

WALLY

Seeing Sean appear in the yard was a dream come true. I never imagined he could actually find me…but he did. He knew exactly where I was, and he came for me. I should've known he would.

He promised.

But how was that possible? I'd heard rumors of such things, and while Sean was in the shower, Doc and Jase were talking about fated mates and destiny… But did that really exist? Could that be what was happening to us? I wanted to believe so, so badly, but the logical part of me said that if I was questioning it, we weren't.

It was probably just the stuff of fairy tales.

With a deep inhale, I let the deliciously comforting scent of Sean fill me up as my eyes drifted shut. Instantly, I was in a different time. A time when I was a whole man, and Sean was wide awake, naked as the moment he shifted, and ready for me.

My standard fantasy began to play out right in front of me.

Sean reached for his cock and started to stroke it before taking mine in his soft but strong hand. Then he'd hold us together, using his big fist to get us both off while kissing me breathless.

It was a dream I had nightly, but now it was closer to becoming a reality someday because he was back. He found me and was lying right beside me. Even in my sleep, as I rubbed my hand over his chest and slipped it under his sweats to feel the massive rod hiding below, it seemed like it was really happening. Like Sean and I could be together as lovers…a family, even.

But not while I was a wallaby. There was no real future for us if I couldn't give him what should be his. If I couldn't be the man he deserved. He needed a man, not a beast.

And right now, that's all I was, my skin nowhere to be found.

My cock was full as I aligned my body with his, adding a new element to the fantasy by sliding lower until my mouth was hovering above his giant dick. My fingers combed through the hair on his thighs then up to his chest before my tongue darted out and scooped up the bead of fluid seeping out.

Sean's fingers locked in my hair as he breathed out my name, lifting his hips to push farther into my mouth. I didn't make him wait. I sucked him fully in, not stopping until his head was pressed firmly against the back of my throat and my tongue was curled around his shaft. After just a few seconds to get used to his size, I pulled off to the tip and then quickly pressed back down, taking him as far as I could in long, slow strokes. His shaft seemed to get even thicker with each pass I took, and when I knew he was about to blow, I reached for my own dick and pumped it in time with my mouth, bringing us both to orgasm at the same time.

"Fuck, Wally!"

I opened my eyes and saw Sean looking down at me. His fingers trailed down the side of my face and curled around the back of my neck. With his cock still in my mouth, resting limp on my tongue, I merely hummed out a response.

His eyes went wide as he seemed to become fully alert. "You're human!"

What? I shook my head, trying to clear it enough to determine if I was still dreaming or if I'd actually woken up…in my skin. "I am?"

He smiled and reached for my shoulders, gently pulling me up over his body. "You are."

"And I'm awake?" I still wasn't sure what to believe. Maybe this was a dream within a dream. goodness knew I'd had plenty of those in my lifetime. "We both are?"

He looked around then lightly pinched my ass. "I think so. No mere mortal could have slept through a blow job like that."

Shit, that was real? "You felt that?"

He chuckled and kissed my forehead. "I felt it, I loved it, and I hope to feel it again." At least he wasn't mad at my handsy and mouthy nocturnal adventures. It wasn't as if I asked permission or even pretended to.

I glanced down and saw my human body for the first time in… I didn't know exactly how long. Everything seemed to be where it was supposed to be, and the bruises I had developed in The Lab were completely healed. I looked like me…only slightly less bony from the healthy food Jase and August had been giving me to get me back to my normal weight. "When did this happen?"

Sean's palm rested on the back of my neck and gave a gentle squeeze. "No idea. I woke up to this glorious sight." He grinned. "I have to admit, it was even better than the dream I was having."

"I thought I was having a dream. The same dream I always have, except this time, it was real… And I'm human." I still wasn't a thousand percent sure I wasn't dreaming, but this was too good to let go of, even if it was.

He leaned forward and gently brushed his lips across mine, testing my reaction before coming back and kissing me more thoroughly. "I would have been happy with you in any form, but I'm really, really happy to see you as a human. I was worried that the things that happened before might have… Well, I wasn't sure if you were stuck." His hand stopped on my hip then tugged my body until I was flush on top of his. "And I'm so glad you're safe."

I inhaled deeply and then relaxed against him, not questioning the *how* or *why* too deeply. Really, the *why* made perfect sense. I definitely wanted this time with

Sean as a man, and obviously, my wallaby understood that.

Closing my eyes, I focused my mind and felt him deep within me, content and happy. It was a strange sensation that I had never quite gotten from him before. "I guess I finally had the proper motivation." Or maybe he needed Sean's strength to help him through.

We lay quietly in each other's arms for a while before some of the questions I'd been dying to verbalize couldn't be held in any longer. "Can I ask you a question?"

"Anything. Anytime." Sean's hand slid up and down my back before resting above my cheeks. It was challenging to think while his hand was so close to my ass, but there was no way I was going to ask him to move it.

"How do you really think you found me? I've never been to this place before, so I know I couldn't have told you where to look. But your stallion just knew. How could that be?" His stallion didn't look around the farm at all. He came straight to me in my half assed attempt at a hiding spot.

Sean sucked in a deep breath and slowly exhaled. "I have a theory, but it might be too soon to talk about it."

That didn't sound good.

I shifted my weight and rested my chin on my folded palms so my face was just inches from his. "It's not too soon. Please tell me." Because now I had a nervous belly. This was one of those band-aid moments when it was best to just rip it off.

Or so I thought.

His other arm wrapped around me, and he held me in place as if he thought I might run with his next words. "I think we're meant to be together. My stallion knew exactly where you were because…you're supposed to be mine."

As I spoke, my eyes were locked on Wally's to gauge his reaction. I didn't know if he would believe me or think I was still under the influence of the drugs they pumped me with at The Lab. I wanted him to believe me, to see how real this was. I needed it so badly that I could taste it. And if he wasn't ready, or wasn't there yet, I'd be patient and wait for him.

For a few seconds, he was quiet, processing the idea, but then he nodded. "Yeah, I think so too."

My jaw dropped, surprised this wasn't a bigger deal. "Really? That's it?" I didn't mean for it to come out the way it did, almost curt. But out it came.

He chuckled and kissed my chest, obviously not taking my abruptness as anything other than what it was…me trying to process this all. "Well, there's no other explanation. Besides, from the first moment I saw you, I knew there was something special about you. You're different from anyone I've ever met before, and no matter how this turned out, I know I'll never feel the way I feel with you…with anybody else."

My heart was full of emotion as I leaned forward, brushing a soft kiss against his lips. I didn't mean for it to go beyond that, but Wally clamped onto me and kissed me like our lives depended on it. By the time I pulled back, gasping for air, I knew my life would never be the same, in the very best possible way.

I'd found my mate, the one fate put on this earth just for me. He was safe and surrounded by people who cared for him. We could now begin our happy ever after together, away from the horrors that brought us together in the first place.

Just as my fingertips started to trail down his hip, a loud rumble erupted from his belly.

Wally's gaze snapped to mine and he grinned. "I haven't had anything to eat except grass and veggies in a really long time. I guess I'm kinda hungry."

Smiling wide, I dropped a quick kiss on his forehead then turned us both to the side of the bed and sat up.

My mate was hungry, and that meant I needed to get him fed. Everything else could wait. We had our entire lives to explore each other's physical bodies, but now, I needed to nourish him.

"Well, then, I guess it's time to introduce this side of you to our new friends."

Wally looked confused for a second, and then he groaned. "You're right. They've never met me as a man. That's going to be weird, huh?"

"I think it's going to be wonderful. I can tell they already care about you and that they were worried you would be stuck as your wallaby forever. This will make them beyond happy."

"And weird," he half mumbled.

I got up and adjusted my shorts to make sure I was as decent as possible despite my semi-hard erection. I needed to think of gross things to settle down before they got more than an eyeful. "Not weird at all. They've been trying to get you to shift, right? They want to meet the man behind the wallaby. At worst, it will be slightly awkward." I winked and held out my hand to the very naked and very gorgeous omega in front of me. "But we'll probably need to get you some clothes first."

Not that I wanted to cover up even an inch of his gorgeousness.

Breakfast was not only delicious, but much more interesting than I could have imagined possible. After introductions to the human Wally were made, we all sat down to eggs and muffins and the most delicious home fries I'd ever eaten. Then again, after weeks without real food, I probably would have been just as excited by dry toast.

I reached for another muffin and reconsidered. Nah, it was an exceptional meal. I snatched it up and August looked at me appreciatively. He was soaking up our love for the food he and his mate prepared for us, and that alleviated any of the self-consciousness I felt about over indulging.

Once their young had finished eating and went to go watch their favorite show, Jase and August filled us in on everything they knew about The Lab, and I did the same. I was impressed with how much they had been able to piece together, especially considering how long it took me to figure out what they were doing.

And I had complete access to so much more data than they did.

My heart hurt.

There were so many other innocent people, mostly omegas, being hurt every single day. I was both surprised and impressed to hear their pack was actively trying to stop those monsters.

Speaking of, their pack was intriguing. It wasn't like any I'd ever heard of. They were a mixed group of both shifters and humans and apparently some were fae. There wasn't the obvious hierarchy that most all of the packs I'd known lived by. There was a pack Alpha, of course, but it was different.

And from what little I knew about it, it was working well for them.

Maybe we were brought to this little town for a reason. Maybe this place with these people and this little powerhouse of a pack were exactly where we were supposed to be. Maybe this was our new home.

That stayed in my mind as we cleaned up the dishes and considered what was next for us.

"So." August leaned against the counter, drying his hands with a rooster-covered tea towel. "What's next for you two?"

I looked at Wally, and he shrugged. "I'm still getting used to being able to see over the counter. I haven't thought much beyond a hot shower and brushing my teeth."

Grinning, I reached for his hand and tugged him into my side. "We can get out of your hair today. If one of you wouldn't mind letting me transfer some money from my online bank account, for cash and a phone, we can probably find a hotel in town for a few days until we figure out our next steps."

That was if my account was still available. I'd been careful to disconnect it from everything else when I first saw the evils of The Lab, but that didn't mean they didn't find it. They had power in really high places and controlled so much more than even I knew.

August looked horrified. "No, not going to happen. You aren't going anywhere until you're totally ready. Please, stay here for as long as you'd like." He rubbed his chin. "What I was getting at, is if you are interested in sticking around for a while, I've been planning to hire someone to help with some of the rescue animals." He raised an eyebrow in my direction. "A wild pony, in particular."

My eyes narrowed. "A rescued pony?"

His arms came up to stop my pending tirade. "Easy there, bucko. It's not what you're thinking. She wasn't abused, as far as we can tell. We think her mother died and she spent a lot of time on her own. She's sweet but isn't really comfortable around people or other animals quite yet."

I inhaled deeply then unclenched my shoulders. "Yeah, of course. I'd be happy to work with her."

August relaxed. "Awesome." Then he twisted to better see Wally at my side. "As for you, if you're interested, Korgen, our realtor friend, is looking for an assistant. He said he'll provide training and you can earn commission on referrals. If you want…"

"Yeah, I'll take it!" Wally realized his overenthusiasm and took a deep breath. "I mean, that sounds interesting. I'd be happy to talk to Korgen about it. If it's still available."

August winked. "I'll tell him to stop by later. He's a cool guy. Unlucky in love, but amazing when it comes to getting top dollar for fixer-uppers. He took over the agency a few years ago, and he really fits in here at River's Edge. He just gets the difference between big city real estate and helping people find their forever home."

Wally gave my hand a squeeze. "That sounds wonderful."

I cleared my throat, wanting to make sure we weren't overstaying our welcome. "Are you both sure it's okay for us to stay a little longer? A week or two, tops. I do have money in the bank. I just don't have easy access to it until I get a new ID and replacement bank cards." Which, the more I considered it, was far more complicated than I initially thought.

"Don't say another word." Jase came to me and placed a hand on my shoulder. "You're welcome to stay as long as you want. A few weeks, a few months, whatever. Just make yourselves comfortable and don't stress about a thing. We're happy to have you."

I swallowed hard and nodded. "Thank you. We appreciate that."

EIGHT
WALLY

The sense of relief I felt after talking to Jase and August was immense. I could tell Sean felt it too. He was the kind of alpha who didn't do well with taking advantage of others. Sean was a caretaker, so asking others for help wasn't easy. But after taking a walk on the property to talk, we both decided settling in River's Edge would be good for us.

At least for a little while.

August was a few inches taller than me, but his pre-pregnancy clothes fit pretty well. I still looked like I was wearing someone else's clothing, but it would have to do. And since Korgen knew about my situation, he'd understand my choice of attire for the day. I was in running shorts and a performance tee, as if I were about to go for a jog.

When Sean came out of his shower and saw me standing there, he raked his eyes up and down my body. Suddenly, I did want to exercise, but not by running. I had other forms of exercise in mind. Sudden or not, if Sean was indeed my mate, which I knew in my heart he was, there was no reason to put off the inevitable. And by inevitable, I meant the scorching-hot sex I was already wet and ready for.

"Wow." He gently closed the door behind him, holding the towel together at his waist. "You look...fucking hot."

I grinned. "I've been thinking." I slipped my hand under the waistband of my shorts and gave my cock a nice pull. "We've already wasted too much time."

He dropped the towel to the ground and his huge cock jutted straight out, bouncing a little with the motion. "Agreed."

"So..." I pulled my shorts all the way off and bent my knees so he could get a full view of how slick and ready I was. "If we're really meant to be mates, there's no sense wasting any more time."

As soon as Sean got to the edge of the bed, he dropped to his knees and then pulled me toward him until his nose was pressed right against my balls. With a long inhale, he tickled my sensitive skin with the cool air that passed over it. "Fuck, you smell so good."

A wave of warm slick oozed out of me, pooling on the bed. "Quit smelling and get in me already."

Sean moaned as he licked from the bottom of my balls, all the way up to the tip of my cock. It was just as wet as my hole, and feeling his wet mouth on me was almost too much to bear. I wanted to come but I wanted him inside me. I wanted him to claim me.

Needed him to claim me.

"Please, Sean."

He lapped up as much of my wetness as he could but more kept coming, so he finally gave up and dropped a trail of kisses up my belly and to my chin. "Please what, sweetheart?"

"Please fuck me."

He shuddered and his cock bounced against my thigh. "If you keep talking like that, I might not make it very far."

"I won't say another word if you just hurry up and get inside me." That was a lie and we both knew it. My mouth wouldn't stay shut under such intense circumstances, but he didn't actually want me to be quiet. It was obvious by the way his pupils dilated that he liked when I got a little raunchy. "Just put that big alpha cock inside me and breed me, Sean. Please. I need it."

Without even reaching down to guide himself in, he shifted his hips and lined up the head of his dick to my opening. I tilted just a few degrees before he pushed all the way in, practically splitting me in two in the most delicious way. "I don't want to hurt you...but I know you can take it."

I sucked in a deep breath, breathing through the spike of pain from his sudden impalement. "I can take it... but damn, now I understand the term 'hung like a horse.'"

After a few seconds, he slowly pulled out and then pushed back in, setting a gentle rhythm while he kissed me at the same leisurely pace.

I didn't know where to focus. The pleasure coming from my mouth or the pleasure coming from my ass... or the even more amazing pleasure coming from my cock as Sean's big body bounced on it.

My tongue slipped inside his mouth, teasing his velvety-soft skin before I realized his hand was wrapping around my cock. Part of me wanted to hold back the orgasm that was just seconds from emerging, but a much bigger part wanted to burst all over him and myself. The way he held me in his hand while his body moved against mine, shaking us together in a wave of friction and sweat, was totally surreal.

My imagination was terrible compared to what this reality felt like. Never could I have imagined how full my entire being would be with Sean inside me. He was in my heart and my soul...not just my body. "I'm gonna come, alpha."

His pace on my dick sped up a bit as he whispered in my ear. "Me too, sweetheart. Just let go. I'm right there with you."

Within seconds, my body was convulsing and rocking against him as thick ribbons of come shot into the space between us. And while my channel clenched around Sean's cock, milking his own climax from him, his mouth closed on my neck and his slick teeth dug into my skin.

My whole focus moved to the connection of his mouth on my skin, forming a bond of blood, saliva, and seed as his knot expanded and locked him inside me. It was almost an out-of-body experience as our auras seemed to blend into one and our beasts were entangled in our coupling.

Time didn't exist…nothing did. It was just us and our forever for several long moments.

When his knot softened enough for him to slip out of me, I reluctantly rolled to the side, giving him space to get up, even though I never wanted him to leave.

Sean was still breathing heavily. "So, that was…"

"Yeah." I traced the mark on my neck with my fingers, loving that the evidence of his claim was still there. "It was."

Not wanting to be rude—ruder than we'd been by claiming each other instead of giving the help we'd promised—we quickly showered again after his knot slipped loose, and then we offered to make everyone lunch.

Between the two of us, we managed to put together a decent spread, one that everyone enjoyed. Of course, we left the dessert to Auggie because he was playing around with some new cookie recipes. Those things were made of magic. They had to be. Nothing of the human realm could taste that good.

After lunch was eaten and everything was cleaned up, Sean went to the paddock with Jase to work with the pony while I hung out with Daisy as I awaited Korgen's arrival. Even in my human form, the silly pig and I got along beautifully. She was wonderful.

This entire place was. There was something special about River's Edge, and with each passing moment, I felt more and more sure this was where we belonged.

NINE
SEAN

Cupid seemed like a silly name for a wild pony, but it suited her pretty well. Once you got to know her, she was a sweetheart. And I could see how she could make you fall in love with her. I felt horrible for her beginnings but was thrilled that she found her way to this farm.

At first, I wasn't sure how she'd react to me. Not only was my inner beast significantly larger than hers, but animals had a way of sensing that shifters weren't quite like people, but also not like them either. Surprisingly, she immediately submitted to me and my stallion and allowed me to get closer than Jase had ever gotten.

I wasn't sure if it was me she trusted, or my stallion's size that had her acting the way she was, but I was glad.

It would make things easier for her as she learned to deal with people and became more comfortable in her surroundings.

Fortunately, that didn't take long, and it was almost as if a switch had been turned and she could sense the alpha stallion inside me. She was no longer nervous around me. Instead, she was eager to please and was completely trusting.

Within the first hour, she let me saddle her up and walk her on a lead.

Jase didn't seem the least bit surprised by her response to me, but I'd never worked with a wild horse so I was very surprised and pleased as I continued to work with her. After a few hours of walking her with full tack, she was putty in my hands.

As the afternoon turned to evening, Jase and I both felt bad leaving her in the stable. She wasn't alone out there, but she clearly wanted to follow us back to the house. I almost asked Jase if I could sleep with her, but a flash of Wally in my mind squashed that idea. Besides, the barn was the safest place for her…and I think she knew that.

Jase handed me a water bottle from the cooler as we turned toward the house. "Looks like you've got a new best friend."

I smiled. "She misses her mama and she's scared. I can appreciate that."

He nodded. "Yeah, me too. Just another reason why we're so glad you're here." He glanced at me and raised an eyebrow. "Do you think maybe you'd want to run with her sometime?"

"Could I?" I'd never lived in an area that was so remote my stallion could just run free at any time. "No one will question it?"

"Nah, you're fine. You can follow the river for quite a while before you hit a heavily populated area. Well, as heavily populated as things get here. And even then, I don't think anyone will bother you. I just don't know enough about wild horses to make her feel comfortable around us. And really, the horses that are here were pretty much as trained as they are now when they arrived…or they were here before I was." He laughed. "And unlike you, my best is no help. I'm just a bunny, so she probably wouldn't even see me if I shifted in front of her. And in human form, she's probably not sure what to make of me…"

Fair enough. "In that case, yeah, I'd love to take her out. Maybe tomorrow. After spending so much time running her, I kinda miss being on all fours."

"Does that mean you're going to stick around for a while?" He opened the screen door to the kitchen and gestured for me to walk inside.

I took a long pull of water, emptying the plastic bottle. "I think so. Wally and I haven't talked too much about our long-term plans, but he seems really happy here. If we can find a more permanent place to stay, I see no reason to leave."

Jase clapped a hand on my shoulder. "Well, it's a good thing your mate is going to be working for a realtor, huh?"

My mate. It was the first time someone other than me or Wally had acknowledged our bond, and it filled me with a warm, melty feeling inside. I absolutely loved the sound of it, and for a split second, I considered asking him to say it again. "Yeah, I guess it is."

"What is?" Wally came in through the door with Jase and August's youngest in his arms. "Are you referring to the absolute ridiculous amount of cuteness I've got in my arms here? If so, then I completely agree." He came to my side and gave me a quick kiss on the cheek. "Isn't she the cutest?"

The longing in his eyes was hard to miss, and I knew what he was really asking me. I nodded. "She is. Maybe someday we'll have one just like her."

Wally sucked in a quick breath and smiled. "Yeah, maybe."

Jase stepped forward. "Until then, why don't you let me take her. I'll put her down before we get too close to the witching hour. That's when the claws come out." He gently cradled his daughter in his arms and gave her a kiss on her head. "Thanks for watching her, Wally. We appreciate the help."

Wally sat at the table and pulled a home-baked cookie from the cookie jar that always seemed to be full. "So, really. What were you guys talking about?"

"Hmm?" I was distracted by the way his lips closed over the cookie with each bite. "Oh, when you walked in? Jase asked if we were going to stay in town, and I told him we needed to talk, but if you're happy here, then we certainly could."

The smile that blossomed across his face made something else blossom. "Really?"

I shifted my weight and subtly adjusted my dick so it wasn't jutting straight out. Then I sat down beside him. "Of course. I have nowhere in particular to go, and the people here seem to be kind." I thought about Cupid and how I could help her adjust to her new family. "And we won't have to live in hiding here in River's Edge."

He reached for my hand and held it on the surface of the table. "I'd like that."

"So…I guess that means you'll need to ask your new boss if there are any houses nearby that might work for us."

"I'm guessing it'll make him like me even more if I bring a buyer with me on my first day." He waggled his eyebrows. "Doncha think?"

"He'll love you no matter what." I pulled his hand up to my lips and left a soft kiss there. "Just like I do."

Wally swallowed hard, and I could almost see the wheels turning in his head. But instead of saying anything, he just reached into the cookie jar and pulled out a big snickerdoodle then handed it to me. "Cookie?"

Leaning forward, I took a bite without grabbing it with my hands. "That's good for now, but it isn't gonna sate my real hunger."

Suddenly, all thoughts about houses and cookies and ponies were gone. All that existed in the world were the ropes of desire and urgent need pulling us together.

Wally sensed it too and excused himself from the room to go lay down.

I followed right after, and I guess, technically, what we did could be called laying down—sort of.

TEN
WALLY

My first day of work was exhausting. Beyond exhausting. By the time I left, all I wanted was a power nap—or maybe a five hour nap. Really, any kind of nap would work.

I made copies of flyers, responded to about a million emails from people interested in seeing our listings, and whenever the phone rang, which was often, I had to stop what I was doing and run to the reception desk to answer it. For whatever reason, people loved River's Edge and the surrounding areas as a potential home location, which was fantastic for business.

Just not exactly conducive to leisurely afternoons of collating and filing.

But deep down, it felt amazing to be so productive, to have a purpose that didn't involve being somebody's lab rat.

I was a fulltime student before I ended up in The Lab, so I'd never had a real job before. Sure, I did the random odd job in high school like mowing lawns or raking leaves, but nothing like this with a boss and set hours and a weekly paycheck. And it wasn't even all about the paycheck.

I was earning my own money now, but more importantly, I felt needed, like I was contributing. Was that a little melodramatic for one day on the job? Possibly.

But I didn't care.

In many ways, it was a foreign feeling, to be depended on in that way. Truthfully, I loved it. I wanted to take on every task Korgen could possibly need help with, but he insisted on starting me slow. Besides, there was an open house coming up that he was sure would be packed with prospective buyers, and if that wasn't a diving in with both feet kind of work day, I didn't know what was. I'd only be helping him, of course since I wasn't licensed for anything.

I was still beyond excited for the experience.

And as my first official foray into the world of real estate, I wanted to put my best foot forward. Thankfully, I had amazing new friends to help me make that happen.

August took me to his favorite clothing store, and I got a suit for the first time in my life. In fact, by the time we left the store, I had two suits, three pairs of jeans that were buttery soft but looked like they were painted on me, and a bag full of dress shirts in varying degrees of professionalism. I promised to pay him back multiple times, but he kept insisting that it was something he wanted to do and to knock it off.

I was still planning on paying him back.

"Do you think Sean will like your new wardrobe?" Auggie hefted one of the bags over his shoulder as we walked to his car. "Or does he prefer you naked in bed?"

My face burned as if it were on fire. I was fine with bluntness—I preferred it—but knowing my new friend knew what I was doing with my stallion made me want to climb in a hole.

"Auggie!" I almost stumbled at his comment, but then I laughed. This was my friend. He wouldn't judge. And besides, he had a fated mate, so he knew how it was.

"Well, he does like that look on me, but I think he'll approve of the business attire too."

"How could he not? That suit is fire!" He had a much better sense of style than I did. If I'd been shopping alone, I would have ended up in a polo and khakis… which was not at all right for showing houses, according to August. "And you'll probably want to model those jeans privately, because if he sees you for the first time in public, things might get a little…embarrassing."

"Are you always this dirty?" I'd never had an omega friend that I could have these kinds of conversations with. I didn't know if it was normal or not, but it was definitely fun once I got over the initial bout of embarrassment. I felt like a normal guy…not an omega or an object…or worse, a specimen to experiment on. I was just a guy hanging out with a friend. "But yeah, my guess is I won't get through two outfit changes before he's got me pinned down beneath him."

"I knew it!" Auggie gave me a playful shove on the shoulder. "You're just as dirty as I am. It's impossible not to be when we've got such hot alphas waiting for us at home."

That was definitely true.

Since Sean and I realized we were mates, it was hard to be apart from him. And when we were separated, even by just a few walls, my thoughts were always centered around him. And I was okay with that.

I never thought I'd have a person who consumed my life…in a good way. And now that I did, I was just so grateful to have him. "Speaking of, we should hurry cuz I miss him."

August popped the locks on his car and we loaded up all my bags. "Okay, okay. We'll be there in just a few minutes."

As he said that, the hairs on the back of my neck stood on end. Something felt wrong, and I was immediately on high alert. Instead of getting into the passenger seat, I spun on my heel and looked around, expecting to see one of the doctors from The Lab heading toward me with one of those damn syringes.

"What's wrong?" August came to my side and tried to follow my line of sight. "What are you looking at?"

"I don't know." I squinted against the bright sunlight, trying to figure out what caused the feeling of unease to settle in my gut. "I just felt like we're being…watched."

He quickly scoped out the area then put his hand on my bicep. "Get in the car. We need to go."

"Do you see something?" I climbed inside and slammed the door behind me, desperate to get back to the house.

"No." August hopped into the driver's seat and started the car. "But I've learned not to ignore those instincts. If something doesn't feel right, it probably isn't. And we don't need to stick around here to find out why."

He was normally a very cautious driver, but I couldn't help noticing that he drove a little faster as we headed back to the farm. "It was probably nothing."

"Maybe." He took a deep breath as we finally turned down the long drive to the house. "But no reason to tempt fate."

As if he could sense something was wrong, Sean walked out of the house and met us in the driveway. Before the car was even turned off, he had my door open. "Is everything okay?"

"Yeah." I wasn't sure how much I should say, but it seemed like he already knew something was up. "Why do you ask?"

Sean's eyes narrowed as he held out a hand to help me out of the car. "Don't play with me, baby. Tell me what happened."

My eyes automatically rolled as I glanced over to August. "How does he know?"

Auggie just shrugged and grabbed a few bags. "They always know. I have no idea how. Human, remember?"

"Know what, Wally?" Sean grabbed the rest of the bags then stood in front of me, waiting for me to spill.

"It was probably nothing…" I gave him the high-level story and watched his fists clench around my poor bags. I didn't want to hide things from him, not really, but I also didn't want to worry him. He'd been through so much, and he didn't need my drama on top of everything. Not when things were finally settling down for us.

"Those bastards better not be tracking me." He was seething as he adjusted the bags so he could put an arm around my waist.

I hadn't thought of that.

I was imagining someone maybe checking out one of our asses or the car or scoping us out because it looked like we had money. If I'd thought for one second it had been about The Lab, I'd have made sure to call and warn him immediately.

My heart dropped as I remembered all the stuff they'd injected in me during my time at The Lab. "Do you think they can? Like, do you think some of that stuff they filled our bodies with could help them do that?" I wouldn't put it past them. If they could do it, of course they would. I just hadn't ever thought about that being a possibility before.

He nodded toward the house and we started walking in. "Maybe. I didn't think about it before, but there were rumors that they injected tracking devices in all the omegas. If they did it to you, they probably did it to me too. And I was a traitor. They did everything they could to make sure I suffered."

Jase appeared out of nowhere and was talking into a phone. He turned back to us as we entered the family room. "Alden's on his way."

ELEVEN
SEAN

Meeting the alpha of the community wasn't at the top of my list of things to do.

Honestly, I wasn't sure how he would react not only to me and Wally as men, but also as shifters. Wally was cute and adorable, and I figured he would fit in. But I was a stallion, and in the shifter realm, we were thought of as big oafs and not much more. And then there was my history with The Lab. Everyone knew how bad the "work" they did there was, and to know I'd one time been a part of that, was something I'd never live down.

I'd automatically dislike me, so I saw no reason why they wouldn't too.

But as soon as I met Alden, all my concerns disappeared. There was just something about him that was warm and inviting. Not once did I feel judged for either my past or my beast. And he'd previously met Wally, just when Wally was a little more hoppy than he was now.

It was clear from the get go that Alden had both my and Wally's well-being as a top priority. He wanted us safe and healthy and comfortable. I'd never had that before…anywhere. And what shocked me the most was that even though we were new to his town and had a history that wasn't admirable, we were part of his pack. It wasn't negotiable. It just was. He fully accepted us as his, and it meant the world to me.

He rubbed his chin with the heel of his hand. "We've been watching a few groups for months now, but you surprised us."

I crossed my arms, inadvertently protecting myself from what I thought was coming. "Sorry about that. I was surprised too. I had no idea where we were going."

Alden laughed. "I think we can all relate to that on some level. But if there are people from The Lab actually following you or Wally, we'll know about it soon. I'm setting up a twenty-four watch on the property."

Wally groaned. "We really don't want to be that much of a burden on everyone."

Alden held up a hand to stop me. "You're not a burden. You're one of us now, and we take care of our own. If there's a threat to you, there's a threat to all of us. I'm not going to allow my family to be at risk." He looked at me. "And I know you feel the same. As long as The Lab is in business, we're all at risk. So, starting now, anyone who comes within a mile of this place will be vetted by us."

"Um…" Wally raised his hand like he was in a classroom. "What about when I'm at work? I have an open house tomorrow that's really important."

I understood that his job gave him a purpose and made him feel like he was contributing, but just hearing him mention going somewhere that would include groups of strangers set my nerves on edge. Office work was one thing. Being out in the open was quite another.

"Skip it." I didn't want Wally exposed to any additional strangers than absolutely necessary. Maybe that made me sound like an alphahole, but I didn't give a damn. I needed my mate safe, and if The Lab was coming for me, then definitely wouldn't be safe just because he was surrounded by people. Especially with an actual sign and arrow pointing his way.

Not. Gonna. Happen.

"I can support us. You don't need to work at all."

I instantly saw the error in my words, but I crossed my fingers that Wally would just let them breeze on past him.

He did not.

Wally had been looking at Alden but he froze and slowly turned to me. "Excuse me?" His voice was so soft that it made it a thousand times scarier—possibly two thousand times scarier.

Oh shit. Clearly, that was the very worst thing to say. "I just mean—"

"Let's get this straight." He lifted a finger and tapped my chest. "You don't tell me what I can and can't do. I want to work, so I will work. If you want to come and sit in the car all afternoon, go for it. But if you expect me to just sit around for the rest of my life and avoid the world… Well, that isn't living." His eyes dared me to argue with him.

But I couldn't. He was right. Based on my omega-istic words, I was in the wrong. So very deep in the wrong.

My jaw dropped, and I was speechless. It took a long moment of everyone staring at me to decide the safest route forward. "I didn't mean it like that. Of course you're your own person, and you can do anything you want. Any time. But——"

The second the B word left my mouth, I just wanted to ask Alden for a shovel so I could start digging my own grave. Because I was dead.

He shook his head. "No buts! I'm going to work tomorrow."

"Yes." I nodded and exhaled deeply. "You definitely are."

He squinted and quirked an eyebrow. "And where will you be?"

I shrugged. "Here. Or with you. Whatever you want."

Alden spoke up and saved me from making it worse, which was apparently my super power for the day. "We'll be there too, Wally. You won't see us, but we'll have eyes on you the whole time. If anything feels off, just whistle and someone will be right there."

Alden's promise made me feel a lot better about the work situation. Not good but better. I wouldn't feel good until he was home safe, in my arms, after the open house was over.

Wally turned to me, waiting for my response.

"Thank you, Alden." I offered my hand again, even though we shook when he first came inside. "Consider me available to you and everyone else at any time. Just say the word."

And I meant it. They were my pack now and whatever they needed I would do. That's what being pack meant.

After the tension during the group conversation, I felt like Wally and I needed some fun.

While I could think of plenty of fun ways to spend the rest of the day naked with my mate, I wanted to give Wally something more special than that—something memorable. Was I possibly trying to make up for my earlier foot-in-mouth situation? Possibly. But in any case, I was determined to take him out on a proper date.

Our first one.

Wally sat in the passenger seat and held my hand as I drove. It was adorable and sweet and made me feel like the luckiest alpha alive. Had you told me as a young adult that something as simple as holding hands would be so powerful, I'd have thought you were clueless. But it truly was. "It was really nice of Jase to let us borrow his truck."

"It was." I switched on the turn signal as we approached a light. Both Jase and August had been nothing but amazing. In a way, we were like rescue animals to them. Not in a condescending way, but in the way that made them want to take care of us and help us get to our new home and life.

Then again, maybe I was thinking too much about it.

"But I think it was as much about us having a date night as it was to make it easier for the pack to keep an eye on us." Alden meant it when he said we were going to be protected. I could feel our pack around us at all times. It was funny, we'd only been accepted as one of his own a few short hours earlier, but the bond was already so strong. the strongest I'd ever felt aside from mine with Wally, and that was a different kind of bond all together.

Wally immediately craned his neck to look out the back window. "Someone's following us?"

"The pack is out there, yes. But they won't be seen. Don't you feel it?" I gave his hand a squeeze.

"I think so. I didn't connect this feeling with that before, but yeah…I feel it. It's more than that though. I think it's the pack thing.

"Yeah, it's the pack thing mostly. I find great comfort in that, but also… I'll be honest, I kinda have that weird feeling of being watched too." I hadn't been able to pick it out until just then and now that I did, it was amplified to the point of complete discomfort. Weird.

Wally laughed. "Well, duh. You are being watched. By the pack. I'm sure that's all that's going on."

I didn't buy it, but I wanted to have a fun night with my mate, so I let that topic drop. "So, I saw a churro food truck when I was out here with Jase the other day."

"Umm, yes!" He pulled our clenched fists to his chest. "I love churros."

"Do you think we should eat some real food first?" I approached the street where the churro truck was parked last time I drove through with Jase and saw a little diner across the street. "That diner looks busy enough that it must be good…but not so busy that we'll have to wait long for a table." It was a fine line that I tried to always be mindful of.

Wally's belly growled right then. "I could go for some mac and cheese."

I parked and we walked to the diner first. Mac and cheese wasn't a given on every menu, but that place looked like it had all the staples. "Then let's get you fed."

TWELVE
WALLY

"That was something, huh?" I took the last bite of my bacon mac and cheese then leaned back in the booth. It was nearly a family-sized portion, and I could see his happiness that I had eaten it all. I was so skinny when I first shifted back to my human form and it was nice to be returning to a healthy weight so quickly. "Not sure what I was expecting…but that wasn't it."

Sean was chewing his pot roast as he cocked his head to the side. "Your food?"

"What?" I looked down at my empty plate then realized I had started a conversation out loud that had been going on in my head…and he had no idea what I was talking about. "Oh, no. I mean with Alden… I wasn't expecting to be welcomed into the pack so completely."

Sean nodded as he wiped his mouth with his napkin. "Yeah, that was something. Even when I was young, I wasn't really part of a herd. We would visit relatives but we were always just guests. I'm not sure I know how to be part of something so…big."

"It's definitely bigger than I thought. If they have enough alphas around to watch us all the time, there must be a lot." I still wasn't comfortable with the idea of having constant security on us, but if it kept those awful doctors from ever finding us, I would deal with it. I'd never survive being held in captivity again…especially now that I had Sean in my life and friends and a purpose. I had so much more to lose now than I ever did before.

Before Sean, I hadn't known how great life could be. And in just a few days of really having him with me, I knew we could never be separated. And our pack? I already loved them. I couldn't explain the hows or the whys of it, but I saw the truth of it. They were mine, and I was theirs. Not in the way Sean and I were each other's, but almost as powerful.

"You got room for one of those churros?" Sean pulled some cash out of his pocket and dropped it on the table. He'd transferred a hefty sum of money to Jase, who had in turn, given him spending cash. At least until new bank cards were issued. It was reassuring to know he had resources if we did need to run.

But I didn't want to live my life on the run. Or to be under constant surveillance. I just wanted for the two of us to be able to live our lives together in peace.

I wanted to stay in River's Edge and be a part of something big. Something that was more than just my little family. "I've always got room for dessert."

He slid out of his booth and held his hand out for mine, helping me do the same.

I didn't need the help at all. That wasn't what it was about. He was just being sweet and kind and a total gentleman. When I stood up, I brought my lips to his ear, "Are you trying to get me naked tonight? Because I have news for you…I'm a sure thing."

He froze, his swallow audible.

I loved that I had that effect on him…that my words alone could have that effect on him.

"Churros first." His voice cracked slightly.

He led me outside and we walked across the street together to order our dessert. He played it cool like my words had no impact on him whatsoever. His jeans told a different story, all tight in the right places.

"I had no idea there were so many options." I had a feeling a lot of them were not close to traditional because they sound delicious and I was on board with that. "This is going to sound awful but…"

"But why don't we get a bunch of things and bring them back to the farm and enjoy them with our friends and their family?" Sean knew exactly where I had been going with my train of thought.

"How did I get so lucky to have such an understanding mate?" I pushed up onto my toes and pressed a kiss to his lips.

"Funny you say that. I ask myself how I got so lucky with finding you all the time. I still don't have an answer, but who needs answers when there are churros?"

The person at the window stepped away, food in hand, and it was our turn. We ordered one of everything, deciding it was the best way to really try the place. It took multiple trips to the truck to get it all there, but the aroma that filled the truck made it clear that the reward was worth the effort.

At least for our edible dessert. Then there was the other kind of dessert on the menu for the night.

"Your jeans are tight. I should fix that." We were driving down the road and the last thing I should be doing was staring at his goods, but there I was, doing exactly that. And the worst part was that I was tempted to do more. Had I not known we were being watched by our new pack, I'd have already begged him to pull over and let me suck him off—a pre-dessert of sorts. But even as my offer to "fix" his erection came out of my mouth, I knew it would have to wait until we were alone…or at least, not under surveillance.

"You are so tempting, my delicious omega."

"Does that mean you'll let me have my naked way with you tonight? Or are you a no hanky panky on the first date kinda guy?" I loved that he took me out on a date —a proper date—even though our relationship was so far beyond that. "Did I tell you that tonight was a first for me? No one has ever taken me out on a real date before. I'm glad it was you."

He started to speed up, and at first, it made me wonder if he thought we were being followed, but then he spoke, and I knew better. "I can't wait to get home and spend the shortest amount of time that politeness will allow with our friends so I can take you to bed and learn all the ways you want to have your way with me."

He settled his hand on my knee. "I'm glad too. One day, it will be a fancy restaurant in a five star hotel." He gave my thigh a squeeze. "I want to spoil you, to give you all the things you deserve and never had before."

"You already have. Just by being mine, you have given me all the things I never knew I could even want and more. I love you."

He turned onto the long drive leading up to the farm.

"And I think ten minutes is long enough." They were churros, not a five course meal…or so I rationalized. "And then I plan to show you just how much I love you."

"All I know is that it can't possibly be as much as I love you, omega mine. There is no love as great."

THIRTEEN
SEAN

Cupid loved to run. If she had her way, I was pretty sure she would spend her days running and eating, with nothing else in between. It was great to see her happy.

Once she saw my stallion, she was a completely different horse. She was playful and relaxed, and as soon as we were off the property and running along the river, she seemed to shed all her fears about being at the sanctuary August and Jase had created. I wasn't sure exactly what it was that had her so connected to me and my beast, but I wasn't going to either complain or second guess it. Her early life had been shit, and seeing her thrive meant so much to not only me, but also Jase and August.

I wasn't able to speak to her, of course, but she could sense when I wanted her to slow down or follow me across the water or when I wanted a break. It was amazing to know that I could help a frightened animal in that way. I totally understood why Jase and Auggie were so committed to rescuing those in trouble.

And I wanted to help them for as long as they'd let me. I wasn't sure how often they needed my help. A rescue farm isn't exactly a for-profit business, and they weren't on a trajectory to grow significantly. Really, the best case scenario would be that the number of animals who needed to be rescued would go down, but that was unrealistic to hope for.

But even part time volunteer work after I got my career back in gear would be an amazing way to spend my free time.

When we got back to the farm, I took Cupid in and shifted in front of her so she knew she was still safe. After spending another hour brushing her out and making sure she was fed and watered, I went to the house wearing just a pair of shorts. I scented like…well, horse…so there was no point in wearing more if a shower was in my immediate future.

Wally was sitting on the steps, waiting for me as I approached.

I looked around to make sure nothing seemed out of place. "Is everything okay?"

"Yeah, I've just been thinking." His serious expression made me nervous. I wasn't sure what was bothering him.

I dropped onto the step beside him, close enough for our knees to touch but still giving him space. "About what?"

He sucked in a deep breath. "I'm ready to try to shift again."

I'd been worried about him being in his skin for so long. I understood the whys of it, of course. But it wasn't good to keep our beasts in for too long.

"Oh, okay. That's great." I placed my hand on his thigh and gave him a gentle squeeze. "Do you want to try it now?"

He looked over at me, vulnerable and scared. It broke my heart. "But what if I can't shift back?"

"You'll be able to. Now that you're not in a desperate situation, and we know everything works the way it's supposed to, I don't think you'll have any trouble changing between forms." And if he got stuck again, we'd figure it out. I just didn't want him to know I thought it was a possibility. My mate was scared enough as it was.

He swallowed hard and looked straight ahead, silently considering whether I knew what I was talking about or not. And the reality was that I didn't. Not even close.

But I did believe he had the strength to do anything he wanted. "No matter what, I'll be right beside you. And if that means I'm cuddling up with your wallaby for a few nights, that's okay too." I winked and leaned against his shoulder, hoping that by mentioning it was okay with me if he got stuck, he might feel a little better. I'd certainly put my foot in my mouth with him several times before. "So, we doing this?"

He stood up and pulled his shirt over his head. "Yup, let's do it."

I didn't want to pressure him, so I dropped my shorts as I shifted into my stallion and then backed away, allowing him to change at his own pace.

"I'm gonna do it." He hopped a little as if psyching himself up for the change. "Easy peasy."

My soft neigh was the only sound I offered as the sun set behind my beautiful omega. His eyes were locked on mine as he shook out his shoulders, naked as the day he was born and waiting for his animal to appear.

The seconds seemed to be passing in slow motion, but after just a few minutes, my man disappeared and his wallaby appeared. He just needed to let his fear go, which was easier said than done.

I was so proud of him.

I lowered my head so he could get a better look.

The wallaby hopped over and nuzzled my head. It was just as sweet and powerful as when we were both human. I could feel the connection, just as alive and strong as ever. After a long moment of learning each other's animal scents, it was time to run.

I galloped to the tree line then looked back to see if Wally was following. He was at my flank, ready for more. Not sure how fast or how far a wallaby could travel, I headed to the river at a casual trot, making sure he was always clear of my heavy steps. Within a few yards, Wally hopped right past me, leaving me in his dust.

Okay, I guess he wants to run…

I took off after him, keeping at a safe distance but staying at his pace. I estimated we were moving at least twenty or twenty-five miles per hour, and it felt amazing. His wallaby was an amazing creature, and witnessing how graceful and smooth he moved was exciting. He was also the most adorable creature I'd ever seen.

By the time we made it back to the house, we barely slowed down enough to shift into our skin before I was pulling his naked body against mine. If we weren't guests in a house with children, I would have taken him right there on the lawn. But since we needed to be good houseguests, I dragged my omega inside to show him just how much I loved him…and how turned on I was after getting to run with him and our animals.

Luckily, we didn't run into anyone as we ran naked through the house to our room. And as soon as the door was closed, Wally was climbing me like a pole. The sweet aroma emanating from him made me harder than ever, and when I finally sank into his wet hole, I knew I was home.

Home with my mate. Regardless of where we were physically, he'd always be holding my heart and soul emotionally.

FOURTEEN
WALLY

Working was as much fun as not working. But as the weeks passed, it took more and more out of me just to make it through the day. I pumped myself full of vitamin C and tried to eat healthy, but I still found myself dragging by three o'clock every afternoon.

Sometimes even earlier.

On the days that I had to work, I'd sacrifice my lunch time for a granola bar and a quick nap in the break room. It was worth it to get the extra sleep, and thankfully, Korgen didn't seem to mind at all. Between my amazing mate, my job, and the lack of new threats in our world, life was pretty great.

Until I started puking.

At first, it was just an icky feeling that would hit me at random points throughout the day. But then it became more and more often, and I started to get worried. A similar feeling had hit me a few times when I was at The Lab. Since I had no idea what was wrong with me or what they did, I was nervous about what it meant.

"You okay?" August came out to the porch with a cup of tea in each hand then offered one to me.

"Yeah, just a little…blah." I wrapped my hands around the warm mug and blew on the steam. "I might be coming down with something."

He eyed me over his mug. "Yeah, I think I had that too…for nine months."

"Wha—" I shook my head and rested the mug on my thigh so I didn't spill it. "You mean…"

"Have you taken a test?"

I shook my head. "No…you think I should?" I'd been so worried that I had some kind of Lab induced disease that I hadn't even bothered to look at the most obvious explanations. Tiredness plus pukiness should've led me on a straight path toward pregnancy. But no—I had to bite off trouble and vear down *the 'of course it's something horrible'* path. Thank goodness for friends like August.

He smiled and stood up. "Come with me."

I was sitting against the headboard when Sean came in from his shower. He'd been helping out more and more on the farm and even went on a few home evaluations with Jase to interview future adoptive families. He was thriving doing this work, and I crossed my fingers he could turn this into a forever gig.

"Hey, sexy." He was rubbing his hair with a towel before tossing it into the hamper. "How was your day?"

"Well, it was…interesting." I swallowed hard, clenching the plastic stick in my fist.

"Interesting…good?" He sat down on the bed, facing me, with his leg bent beside mine. "Or interesting bad?"

"I think it's good." I shrugged. It was good in theory, but knowing the mess my body could be in, I was apprehensive, too. "I hope you do too."

He stared at me for a second then placed his hand over my closed fists in my lap. "So are you going to keep me in suspense forever?"

I sucked in a deep breath and then held up the plastic stick so he could get a better look. "It's positive."

"It's positive?" He took it between his fingers like it was made of fine porcelain. "So you're…"

"We're…pregnant." I bit the inside of my cheek and looked into his eyes. "Is that okay?"

"Okay?" He pulled me onto his lap and kissed me hard on the mouth. "It's amazing."

"It is amazing!" I finally allowed the emotions inside me to flow…as well as the tears I'd been holding in for hours. "I'm so glad you're happy. I've been wobbling between ecstatic and nervous all afternoon not knowing how you'd feel."

Sean's strong hands held me tight against his body. "Nothing makes me happier than to know that we are gonna have a baby. A combination of me and you in one perfect package."

I tried to wipe my tears away but Sean beat me to it, kissing my cheeks until I had no reason to do anything but kiss him back. "I know we've already made a baby…but maybe we can try to make another one?" I'd deal with Doc and my apprehensions later. Right now, I wanted to celebrate with my mate.

He smiled against my lips. "Not sure it works that way, but I'm willing to give it a try."

Sean hadn't gotten dressed yet, so I took advantage of his state and shimmied off his lap and onto my still-flat belly so I could suck this thick cock into my mouth. He was just starting to thicken up, but as soon as my lips closed over his velvety skin, he was rock-hard and filling my throat with his entire cock.

I swallowed around him, loving how full he made me… in every way. My tongue curled around his shaft as I pulled off to take a breath then slowly pushed back down until my nose was buried against his silky soft skin. His scent had already become the most soothing aroma in my world. One whiff of his musky clean skin was enough to get slick pouring out of me.

"You feel too good, sweetheart."

Before he could come, I pulled off and wiped my mouth. "I need you inside me."

"Yes." I practically flew through the air as he shifted me to the mattress and spread me open.

My body was made for Sean's, and I didn't need any prep. At any given moment, he could slide right into me and I would stretch to take every inch of him. This was no exception. Desperate need to feel him overtook me as I pulled my knees to my shoulders and invited him in.

As always, my whole body reacted to his immense size by arching toward him, moving in such a way to accept him in. Once he was fully seated within me, his mouth closed over mine, kissing me hard as he began to move in and out of me.

Ecstasy and happiness flowed through me as I felt Sean's cock get even bigger before emptying inside me. His seed mixed with my own slick, and he was swimming inside me. I couldn't hold back any longer. My hand flew to my dick, and I pulled it just once before shooting a thick stream between our bodies as I rode the wave of pleasure Sean always brought me.

Sean's knot expanded, locking him inside me as I finally relaxed against his heated skin. "I love you, Sean."

His arms closed around me, and he pressed his lips to the side of my head. "I love you too, sweetheart. Now and forever."

Knowing I was going to become a dad was a heady feeling. Not only did it solidify the family unit Wally and I were building together, but it also forced us to commit to staying in River's Edge. Which I was grateful for. I needed the kick in the ass to allow me to accept what I'd already known: this was where we belonged.

Having a strong group of alphas looking out for Wally was a huge relief, especially since having some independence from me was important to him. I never wanted to be separated from him, but I respected that he loved his job and wanted to make it on his own. Just as he respected the same about mine.

But that didn't mean I wasn't looking for excuses to hang out with him as often as possible. If he told me he wanted to work with me and the animals, I'd have gladly shown him the ropes. It wasn't his calling, but the idea of spending every day with him sounded like a bit of heaven on the farm to me. Did that mean I was head over heels for him? Definitely, and I was okay with that.

"Knock, knock." I leaned inside the office and looked for Wally. "Can I come in?"

Korgen was at his desk, taking a bite of a sub sandwich. "Yeah, of course. Wally is in the breakroom."

I walked through the front office and entered the breakroom, surprised to find Wally sprawled on the couch with a half-eaten granola bar precariously positioned between his fingers. My first instinct was to pull out my phone and snap a picture because he was so cute.

And then I heard a voice coming from the front office that had my blood running cold.

"I think his name was Wally. He said he knew of a house I might like. Is he here?"

Korgen was a good man and had obviously been informed of the situation Wally and I were in. "He's not available today. Called in sick. But I'd be happy to help you."

Without even waking him, I slipped my arms under Wally's back and knees and lifted him up. We needed to get out of there quickly.

His arms instinctively wrapped around me but his eyes stayed closed, even as he inhaled deeply and smiled. "Sean."

"Yes, baby. I'm here, but we've gotta go." I went immediately to the back door and stepped into the employee parking lot. There was no time for discussion. They found us.

Two guys I recognized from the pack were immediately on us. "We've got a car around the corner. Get inside and we'll take it from here."

I didn't look back as they ran inside. I trusted they had the situation under control. Obviously, they knew what was happening almost before I did, so after Wally and I were safely in the car, I was able to address Wally's sleepy confusion and explain what little I knew.

I despised the look of fear in his eyes as I told him what had happened, but he needed to know. We weren't as safe as we had been lulled to believe.

The Lab was after us. It was no longer a hypothetical. They found us.

"So, they were trying to kidnap Wally?" He looked between me and Alden, who was driving the large SUV.

"We're not sure." Alden glanced at us through the rearview mirror. "He's been detained and is getting interrogated now. We'll find out what the hell he wants with you, Wally, but until then, we'd like to ask you to be careful."

My response was instant, leaving no room for discussion or misunderstanding. "He will be."

"*We* will be." Wally narrowed his eyes. "If they want me, they want you. So if I'm on lockdown, you are too." He was right, but I didn't care about nearly as much about myself as I cared about him. He was carrying our baby, and his safety was my top priority.

"Thank you." Alden nodded as he turned down the driveway to the farm. "But a full lockdown here probably isn't necessary. Just stick together when you leave the property. And your security detail will be more visible for a while."

Alden's phone rang just as we pulled to a stop. Instead of answering with the SUV's Bluetooth system, he answered directly with his phone so we couldn't hear the other end of the call. All we could hear were his grunts and single-word questions until he sighed heavily and disconnected the call.

"Everything okay?" Wally's palm tightened on my thigh. "Did he talk?"

Alden's gaze connected with mine, silently asking for permission to speak freely.

I nodded slightly, hoping Wally didn't notice.

"The good news is that we're sure he was alone. We tracked his scent for fifty miles and there wasn't anything else mixed with his. So, he wasn't part of a bigger group."

I swallowed hard. "And the bad news?"

"He had a poison tooth. Before we got any real information out of him, he bit into it and was gone." Alden looked at me. "And he wasn't carrying a phone or any ID when we found him, so we're back to square one."

My blood went cold. That same tooth could have easily been used on my mate.

Wally grabbed my hand as I opened the door to get out of the SUV. "Will more be coming?"

I tugged him toward me and helped him out. "Maybe. But now we know who we're looking for. And it's just as likely he was a scout that had no idea if you were here or not. So, let us worry about who might be out there, sweetheart."

I had enough worry for the both of us and then some.

"He's right." Alden met us on the other side of the vehicle. "We'll set up a wider perimeter, so you should be fine while you're in town. We'll all be watching for unexpected visitors, but it doesn't seem like he had backup on the way or he would have held out a little longer."

SIXTEEN
WALLY

Turned out, I was a terrible homebody. I thought it would be fun to be holed up at the farm with Sean all day…but after a week, I was over it. I wanted to go to work, to be productive.

And even though we were "allowed" to go to town, it didn't feel safe doing so just because I was bored and wanted to check out the second hand store or get more churros. Staying home was the right thing to do, even if it was driving me bonkers.

As time passed and there continued to be no indication that any other scouts or Lab people were heading to River's Edge, I was able to go back to work. And I was just in time because Korgen won the contract for a new condominium building that overlooked the river and he had ten showings a day. According to Korgen, this condo project was a sign that the small town was on its way to being less…tiny. People saw it as a place that not only could, but would thrive. I loved that.

Since he was also an alpha shifter, Sean felt confident he'd be able to handle any threat or situation that did come up. My poor alpha would have probably felt more comfortable if Korgen was mated, but August and Jase both assured us he was completely respectful and could be trusted with our lives. And it wasn't even jealousy that plagued Sean. There was something inherently protective inside a mated alpha, and Sean wanted that for me every second.

By the time the worst of my morning sickness had passed, I was eager to visit Doc again to get an update on the baby. He'd been so great in reassuring me at my first appointment. But I was still worried. Looking good when your baby is the size of the head of a pin was much different than things looking good when they were the size of your fist.

Sean met me at the model condo, and I gave him the grand tour. "And this is the second bedroom. Some people will use it as an office or guest room, but…I think it's the perfect size for a nursery."

He quirked an eyebrow. "You think so?"

"Yeah, don't you?" I ran my finger along the windowsill. "And there's a beautiful view of the river."

He pulled me against his chest, and we looked out the window together. "I was envisioning a little house with a stable…but I guess it's not too far to visit Cupid at the farm."

I bit my lip and looked at the side of his face. "So you like it?"

"Of course I like it." He turned me in his arms so we were facing each other. "And if this is where you want us to start our family, I'm in. Wherever you are is home. The rest is a bonus."

The tiny baby in my belly chose that moment to press my bladder and remind me how badly I needed to pee. "And speaking of bonuses, this one thinks my bladder is the perfect resting spot."

After asking Korgen to prepare a contract for us, we headed out. I was on top of the world for a few minutes, but then reality sank in again.

Once we were in the car, I tried not to think about any potentially bad news we could get from Doc. But it wasn't easy. As much as I hated to think about it, there was a lot that could go wrong. All the testing and experiments The Lab did to my body might have had long-term effects that I wouldn't know about until the worst happened. The fact that I was able to get pregnant was a miracle, and hoping for a healthy baby seemed like I was being greedy, but deep down, that was all I really wanted.

I just wanted to know that my baby would have a healthy, happy life.

As we waited in the exam room, Sean could sense that something was wrong, but his initial assumption was way off. "If you're not 100% sure about this condo, we can wait. There's no rush to decide right now."

I sighed. "No, it's not about that."

He stepped in front of me, standing between my spread knees. "Then what is it?"

I placed both hands over my belly, cradling it protectively. "What if something's wrong?"

"Why would anything be wrong?" Sean covered my hands with his. "There's no reason to believe there's a problem. Doc will do his thing, and if there's something we need to be worrying about, we'll start worrying then. Deal?"

I nodded even though I couldn't commit to not worrying. It was part of my nature.

Without the threat to our lives hanging over my head, 100% of my worrying capacity was focused on this baby. When Doc finally came in with his stethoscope in hand, I was ready to burst. "Please tell us everything's okay."

"What?" Doc looked confused, turning between me and Sean. "Is there something I don't know about?"

Sean shook his head. "No. Just normal new-dad fears. Hopefully you'll have some good news to help alleviate some of those."

"Oh, gotcha. I have just the thing." Doc nodded knowingly then turned on the sonogram machine beside the exam table before helping me lean back. "Let's get a look at this little one to put all our minds at ease."

I tried to take slow and even breaths so nothing would be jostled as Doc dragged the slicked-up wand across my belly. Intellectually, I knew that I wasn't going to affect the image with a shaky breath, but I still couldn't help holding extra still just to make sure we got a clear view.

Doc clicked on the monitor several times before he finally leaned back on his stool and nodded. "Okay, everything looks great." He pointed to a little blob that seemed to be pulsing on the screen. "That right there is a perfectly healthy heartbeat."

A huge weight lifted off my shoulders, and I felt an immense amount of relief wash over me.

And then he pointed to another blob. "And here's our second heartbeat."

"A second heartbeat?" Sean leaned closer to the screen and squinted to get a better look. "Two babies?"

"Two babies." Doc changed the contrast and outlined a hazy circle around each blob. "Fraternal twins. See, these are the separate amniotic sacs."

"But they're healthy? Everything looks good?" Now Sean sounded like the worried one, while I was just elated by the good news.

"You can't tell…" I felt silly asking the question, but I wanted to know. "I mean, is there a way to know what kind of shifter they are?"

Doc smiled and slid his hands into his pockets. "I wish there were. I had the same questions about my own young, but it's gonna be a while before you know for sure. But I'll run a few tests. If I see anything noteworthy, you'll be the first to know."

I wiped away the happy tears on my cheeks. "We'll love them no matter what."

"Damn right we will." Sean kissed me on the nose first and then on the lips. "I love you, sweetheart."

"Me too, alpha." I remembered we had an audience and needed to keep it G-rated. "Um, I guess we should get out of here."

He winked. "Yeah, good idea."

Doc had his back turned to us as he washed up. When it was safe to turn back, he handed me a few papers. "Here are some pamphlets on what to expect, but you know you can call me at any time."

"Thanks, Doc." We didn't waste any time before we were on our way out the door. "We'll talk soon!"

SEVENTEEN
SEAN

Wally's sex drive was off the chain.

We were able to move into the condo after a ten-day close, and as soon as we had ultimate privacy, he was riding me every chance he got. Which was fine by me. I loved watching him move with only his growing belly between us.

We filled the home with not only hand-me-down gifts from our friends, but also some vintage treasures from the antique store in town. I had the money to buy new, but Wally loved the idea of making the new space feel cozy and lived in. I had to admit that he was right about the joy in that came from mish-mashing styles.

It all worked together and gave us a safe and cozy abode.

We were in our own little bubble of love and joy and anticipation. So when I got a text from a member of the pack that said someone had been caught snooping around the farm, I was caught off guard by the reminder of the evil that lurked out there.

And more than that, I was pissed. Pissed at myself for letting my guard down and putting my mate at risk… and even more pissed at our past that wouldn't leave us be. I had allowed myself to get distracted into complacency and that put my mate in danger. If anything ever happened to him, I'd never forgive myself.

Those bastards from The Lab would not ruin the only happiness I'd found in my entire life. I would die before I let that happen. And sure as shit, I'd be taking them with me.

With total disregard for any witnesses, I left my sleeping omega and bolted out the door. I wasn't going to leave Jase and August with the mess of dealing with the threat to my family.

They had a family too.

I went straight to the river, shifting out of my clothes and my skin before my foot even hit the water. Running on all four would get me there faster than taking our vehicle because following the river was a direct line to the farm. I didn't have the time or patience to go the long way.

I needed to get to the threat and to annihilate it.

The distance between our place and the farm wasn't far, but every step felt like it took an eternity. Like I was going in slow motion, in a movie that was moving at a pace perfect for dramatic effect and not for action. It only made me run faster. I wanted to be the one to beat the shit out of whoever had been threatening those I cared about. And after he was a pile of goo, I'd find out who sent him so we could preemptively deal with them next.

I refused to let my young be born into a world where they were constantly in danger.

The farm was mostly dark when I arrived, and it was quieter than I expected. Almost too quiet. Nothing about it felt awake. My heart started to race as the fear began to settle in. Something wasn't quite right.

There were no unexpected sounds or scents coming from the barn, so I went to the front door and shifted as I tried the knob. It was locked, which didn't make any sense, so I banged on the door, worried that my friends were in trouble. "August. Jase. Are you okay in there?" They rarely locked the door, unless that was just because they had guests. But even still, it felt wrong being locked up like this.

Jase pulled the front door open, wearing nothing but a worried frown. "Sean, what's wrong? Is Wally okay?"

"He's safe at home." I poked my head inside. "Where is that bastard? I want a piece of him before you guys are through with him."

Jase looked more confused than he should have and my stomach dropped. "What are you talking about? Who do you want a piece of?"

A ball of dread started to form in my belly, but my brain didn't connect any dots yet. "The guy you found here. From the text?" I reached for my phone but remembered I was naked too. "Who sent me the text?"

That was when things started to click. They didn't say who they were. I'd been so ready to jump into action that I didn't look for any red flags, and now, as I watched Jase's expression morph into panic, it was clear I was very wrong.

Jase's eyes went wide, and he was already reaching for his phone, making the connection that I wasn't able to —or was in too much of a hurry to do something to bother with. Guilt began to flood me. "Fuck, Sean. We have to get to Wally."

I heard him talking to someone, but I didn't stick around to find out who. I was back on four legs and running straight through the woods to my house. If someone had lured me away from the condo just to get to Wally, I'd never survive it.

I wouldn't want to.

Wally needed me. Our young needed me. I had to get to my family before it was too late. I should've seen the text for what it was. This was my fault, and if anything happened to them, I'd never forgive myself—ever.

My legs pumped harder and faster than should have been possible, but adrenaline was a powerful fuel. And when a jolt of fear registered in my core, I knew it was from Wally. I could feel him—his connection to me strong enough that it was almost as if I were right beside him. It was like my dreams back at The Lab with its intensity and it nearly had me falter.

My mate was in trouble, and I wasn't there to help him. Slowing down due to his emotions only put him in greater danger. I refused to let him down.

My nostrils flared and foam poured from my lips as I pushed myself as hard as I could. I made it to the parking lot in time to see Vincent, the man who'd hired me at The Lab, dragging Wally toward a van. Wally wasn't struggling, instead making himself dead weight, buying time for our pack to help…for me to help. Where did he think I was? Did he think The Lab already had me? Did he think this was the end and he was going back? Only this time, he wouldn't be alone. He'd have our baby with him.

No fucking way was that going to happen.

I ran straight for them at full speed. Wally saw me coming and held my gaze until I was just a car's length away. He was trying to tell me something. I wanted to stop and decipher it, but my need to get to him and destroy Vincent was too great.

Wally, my brave, strong mate, closed his eyes and shifted instantly. When he needed his beast most, he came out in a flash. Wally disappeared from the disoriented man's grip and hopped out of the way. I wasn't sure what they did to him in The Lab in his final days there, but the shock on Vincent's face told me he didn't believe he could shift anymore, at least not that easily.

I reared up on my hind legs and crashed down on Vincent with all my weight. Had I managed to get my feet in the right spot, it would've been the end of him, but I landed on one arm and leg. He bellowed out in pain and collapsed beneath me, but as hurt as he was, he managed to reach for a gun holstered under his shattered arm. I kicked it out of his grasp, trying to figure out what to do next. As much as I wanted Vincent eviscerated from this planet, he had information we could use to help protect countless others..

Two wolves and a cougar appeared in my periphery, shielding Wally from the fight. I was glad because with each breath he took, the more I saw this man wasn't going to talk—ever. He spent years torturing and facilitating the torture of others. And why? For profit. Even if we used horrific tactics, which we wouldn't, he'd wait us out.

He was useless to us alive and dangerous beyond belief.

Had I been human, there would be a process, one I had to file. But I was a shifter and shifter laws were on my side. He was harming my true mate, threatening his life and the lives of our young. He needed to be put down.

I reared up again and dropped right on his chest, ending the life that had ended so many others.

There was a flash of regret for not getting any information from him, but it was short-lived knowing that that would never have really happened. More than anything I wanted every person who worked for The Lab to die, making it impossible for them to hurt even one more shifter. If that meant we had to take them down one asshole at a time, that was what we'd do.

Violence had never been a part of my life, the way it was with some beasts. But protecting my family was and always would be. And now that I was part of River's Edge Pack, that family extended beyond just Wally and our babies.

It was the entire pack. I would do anything to protect them as they would to protect us. That's what packs did, and I was honored to be part of this one.

EIGHTEEN
WALLY

I knew I'd be bigger with twins than if I just had one baby growing inside me, but I was huge. Like back out of the grocery aisle to let the preggo through kind of huge. I wasn't sure how I wasn't toppling over every time I stood up.

There were times I looked down, saw my belly moving from their kicks and had no doubt that two full-grown stallions were about to burst out of me. And the scary part was that I was only halfway through gestation. I was already at the stage where I could no longer see my dick. At the rate I was going, I was pretty sure I wasn't going to see the living room rug soon.

"You're right." Doc flipped through his paper notes and then punched something into his keyboard.

"You're measuring a bit larger than what I was expecting."

I tensed, clenching Sean's hand even tighter. "Is that bad?" I'd made the mistake of joining an online expectant parents group, and I'd be lying if I said it didn't make me an anxious ball of worry over all the things that could possibly go wrong.

"No, not at all." He didn't seem overly worried, so I tried to keep calm. "But it does bring me to something else I wanted to talk to you about."

"I knew it." I started breathing fast, struggling to fill my lungs. "It's me, right? Something's wrong with me."

Now it was Sean's turn to squeeze my hand like I might float away. "That's not it, right, Doc?"

"No, no, no." Doc waved away our fears. "Nothing like that. It's just that I talked to some colleagues who are familiar with wallaby shifters, and they led me to believe you might develop a pouch."

I'd wondered about that, but figured that having a stallion mate would mean my pregnancy might not be typical of my kind. I knew of at least one wallaby who never had a pouch after quite a few pregnancies, so that had been one of the least of my concerns.

My hands immediately closed over my belly, feeling around for a pouch that I knew wasn't there, just in case he saw something I didn't. "What does that mean? Should I be worried about it?"

I could see the fear forming on Sean's face, but he didn't say a word. He was being strong for me. Just like he had the night that Vincent came for me. He said I was the brave one, using my wallaby to escape. But there was nothing brave about me. I froze until I saw his eyes. It was his strength that saved me, whether he realized it or not.

"Well, you know Holden, of course. He spent a lot of time at The Lab as well." He was one of my new pack members. I'd only talked to him a handful of times, but he seemed nice. Everyone did. "His pregnancy was healthy and all…but there were some unexpected aspects."

"Unexpected how?" Sean's voice cracked, betraying the strong facade he was trying to project.

I loved Doc, I really did. But his bedside manner today was lacking. I needed him to pull off the bandaid instead of this slow reveal garbage.

"Not in a bad way." Doc held up his hands. "But his DNA was altered in a way that made his baby… Well, we're not sure what kind of shifter the baby will become."

I didn't know what experiments he'd been part of, but I could believe that. They were relentless and cruel in what they did to us. Messing with our DNA seemed like the least of it.

Sean's grip loosened a bit. "What does that mean for us? Will our babies be wallaby or horse?"

My mate and I had already discussed it, and we didn't care what kind of beast they were as long as they were healthy and safe. Still, it would be nice to know, just for fun.

Doc clasped his hands together. "That's the thing. They might not be either."

My jaw dropped open. How could we not know? Because of the DNA?

"Depending on what was done to you…both of you." He looked at me and then Sean. "Your young might be any shifter…or all."

"What?" I gasped. The possibility of our babies not being shifter at all because of recessive genes, was something all shifters had to accept. But multiple animals in one person… How was that even possible? It was crowded enough with just my wallaby and me inside of my thin body. Surely, he was exaggerating.

Not that I was able to ask. I got lightheaded and wasn't able to follow the conversation after that. Whatever that meant didn't compute in my head.

I woke up in my bed with my alpha beside me, trailing his fingers over my exposed belly and humming a tune that sounded familiar but I couldn't place. "We're home?"

"Mm-hm." His fingers continued to draw circles on my skin. "You passed out."

I closed my eyes and sighed. "Sorry. What did I miss?"

"Not much." He tilted his head so he was facing me. "Doc said you and the babies are great, so I'm not worried."

That was good for him, but I was still very much afraid. I expected our visit to Doc to include a talk about me not really needing to eat for three or something like that. Not that I was possibly a mutant like in a comic book about to give birth to a weird ass shifter.

"Are you sure?" I cupped the bottom of my belly, holding some of the weight in my hand. "We don't even know what kind of shifters they'll be."

He smiled. "Well, we know they're gonna be big…and strong. So that's good. And yes, I'm sure, and so is Doc. I wish I could take your worry from you."

I did too.

Closing my eyes, I tried to figure out what kind of shifter would make my belly so big. There was a relief in being able to do that, simply imagining for the fun of it. It meant that I didn't really care about who my young grew up to be. Not that I ever thought they could be a disappointment to me, but I never thought any of this would be possible. "Elephants or hippos would be my guess."

Sean's warm lips landed on my nipple then kissed down to my belly button. "Maybe. But no matter what, we'll have a perfect family. But if we do have an elephant or two we might want to get some place with more of a yard than this condo. Elephants don't really blend as well in the forest."

As if wallabies were any better.

I nodded as a shiver of desire shot up my spine when he tweaked my nipple. "Uh-huh."

His lips continued to drop kisses until he was at the base of my cock. "Speaking of perfect…"

I might not be able to find my dick anymore, but Sean sure could and I nearly came as he licked the precum from my tip.

Being with Sean was like food from the fae. One taste and nothing else would ever be good enough again. No matter what mood I was in or how tired I was, as soon as I felt any part of his body on any part of mine, I was instantly hard and ready to go. Just his warm breath on my cock was could make my head leak and my ass slick.

I wanted my alpha. Now.

My hips lifted just enough that the tip of my cock hit his tongue. As always, Sean moaned and sucked me down his throat, bringing me to the edge of orgasm in seconds. My fingers threaded in his hair as he went up and down, allowing me to fuck his face while his finger sought out my opening.

Sean sucked me until his cheeks hollowed and I couldn't hold back any longer. My balls tightened, and I emptied my load down his throat in record time.

I didn't even allow myself to recover from that one before I got up on my knees and leaned against the headboard, shaking my ass at Sean. "More."

NINETEEN
SEAN

Life was calm.

From every indication, killing Vincent had put an end to the hunt for me. When the pack searched his body, they found a tracker, and Alden took it across the country and destroyed it. Would that keep us safe forever? Probably not. But for now, we hoped The Lab would assume he was searching for far, far away.

Wally and I settled into a domestic routine. Right down to a rotation of take-out meals, depending on the day of the week. Neither of us were very proficient in the kitchen, so it was easier to order in, especially as his belly got too big to use the stove safely.

He complained about his oversized belly, but I loved it. Every day it grew a bit more, and I made sure to kiss every inch of it in appreciation…and appreciate it I did.

As long as it wasn't empty. My mate could get hangry, so I did my best to preemptively avoid that.

As we got closer to Wally's due date, the variety of food he wanted was becoming more limited. Like, mac and cheese from a box and peanut butter and jelly sandwiches. Neither of which required a take-out menu.

"We have hotdogs," I called out to Wally from the kitchen. "Want me to cut some up in your noodles?"

"Noooo!"

I wasn't sure what was so horrific about the hotdogs he picked out at the market yesterday, but I knew better than to ask.

"Oohhhkaaaayyyy." I kept stirring, wondering if I should offer broccoli or just let it go. Letting it go was safest even if Doc did recommend more greens in his diet.

"Aaaahhhhhhh!" Wally cried out but I couldn't tell if it was in pain or in frustration. He was frustrated a lot now that he was at the point where he couldn't pick something up off the floor or stay out of the bathroom for more than thirty minutes at a time.

"You okay in there?" I turned off the stove and went to the family room.

Wally was bent over the sofa with his face buried in the cushion and a puddle between his legs. No, he was not okay. He was in labor. My mate was having our twins…now!

"Holy shit! It's time." It was probably not the most productive thing to say, but he didn't seem to notice, his focus on the contraction that he was smack dab in the middle of.

He moaned something unintelligible as I grabbed my keys and then scooped him into my arms. He was easy enough to lift, even at his size, but getting him through the door was a bit tricky. Not that I was foolish enough to let him know that.

"Just keep those babies cooking for a little bit longer. We'll be at Doc's in ten minutes." I knew that shifters had babies at home all the time, and it was always fine. But Sean was having twins after being a prisoner of The Lab. I wasn't willing to take any chances. We were going to have a doctor assisted birth if there was anything I could do about it.

It took a minute to get him into the car, but once I did, I drove as fast as I could without risking Wally's comfort as he shifted his weight from hip to hip, trying to get past the pain that was shooting through him.

I thought it would be an all-day ordeal. I expected walking and crying and ice chips and soft music. Maybe even a lower back rub or two. I'd seen enough movies to know that giving birth could be a two-day process and that the odds were good he would threaten to never let me touch him again. And obviously, I'd be to blame for all the pain he was in.

But none of that happened.

Doc was waiting for us with his assistant when we pulled up to his office. Wally went directly from the car to a wheelchair to a delivery room. The office looked so small that I hadn't even noticed they had a delivery room. I guess when you're a shifter doctor, you have to be prepared for everything.

And while I was scrubbing my hands, he was being prepped for surgery. Doc promised he wouldn't need it, but that being prepped, it was practically a guarantee we wouldn't need to be. He made a joke about it being like taking an umbrella to a picnic.

But those babies weren't interested in being prepared for anything. They wanted out…asap.

By the time I got to Wally's side, Doc gave me a relieved look. "You're just in time, Papa."

I could sense our children and they were ready. I took Wally's hand in mine and kissed his palm. "You're so close, sweetheart."

He nodded and sucked in a deep breath. "I don't know if I can do it."

I brushed some sweaty strands of hair off his forehead. "You're already doing it, my love."

Doc gave him an encouraging pat on the knee. "Baby A is ready. When you feel the next contraction, push hard, and we'll make some space in there to let Baby B out." He said it as if it was as easy as going to the grocery store and grabbing a gallon of milk.

Even as a bystander, I knew it wasn't.

I watched in fascination as my omega performed a miracle and delivered not one but two perfect baby boys. Especially since they were not small at all. In fact, Doc said they were the biggest twins he'd ever delivered.

But when I held each one in my arms, I knew they were exactly right.

No matter what animal they eventually shifted into, our family was exactly as it needed to be.

"Look what we made." Wally looked up at me, his face both exhausted and full of emotions. "How is it possible we did this? They're so perfect."

"I don't know how you did this. You amaze me everyday with your strength, your bravery, and your ability to persevere. I'm so lucky to have you in my life, sweetheart."

"That's where you are wrong, my love. I'm the lucky one."

I snuggled beside him on the small bed, both of us holding our babes and knew that he was wrong. I was the luckiest shifter on this planet.

(Ten months later)

"I don't want to." I stared at my babies in their high chairs and pouted. "They look so cute like this."

Sean pushed a lock of hair away from Taven's eyes. "They can't see. We have to cut it."

Their golden locks were longer than was reasonable for a toddler. Part of me wondered if their mane was an indicator of their future animal, but I kept that to myself. No need to put pressure on anyone to be anything before they were ready.

"Fine, but you better save every strand so I can scrap-book it."

"Whatever you say." Sean gathered a thick bunch of hair in front of Tobin's forehead and held up the shears. "Does this look right?"

I grimaced. "Not really, but I guess just do it. It'll grow back if it looks bad." I had the camera poised to take their 'after' pictures. "Hurry before I change my mind."

Had it not blocked their vision, and if they allowed us to do anything to keep it back, I'd have caved. But now that they were mobile, they needed to be able to see without an obscured view. It was fascinating to me how some babies had no hair and others, like ours, had buckets full since birth.

Sean sucked in a deep breath and then clipped the scissors in a straight line. "Okay, there. The first cut is the hardest."

I finally exhaled and snapped a photo. "Okay, you're right. It's nice to see those big, green eyes."

Cringing the entire time, we managed to get through our boys' first haircuts and then their baths. By the time we got them down for a nap, I was just as exhausted as they were.

But I had other bed-related activities in mind. Some that were even better than a nap.

Sean cleaned up the kitchen while I rinsed off and slipped into bed, waiting for him to join me. My cock was hard, so I casually stroked it, not wanting to waste a minute once he was ready.

Since the boys were born, our lovemaking schedule had slowed down to a humble two times per day. But now that they were starting to take longer naps, we were able to really take our time, enjoying every second of our time together.

I never realized how happy I could be with a partner. I guess I never let myself believe I could find someone who loved me wholly and completely for me. Not because there was anything to gain by being with me. Just for the pure joy and happiness and love of being together.

That was the best way to describe what Sean and I shared.

Our animals couldn't be any more different, and we both had varied backgrounds, but we fit together perfectly...like the broken pieces of a mirror, easily locking in place once we were nudged in each other's direction.

And not only was the emotional satisfaction more than I could have ever imagined possible, but the physical ecstasy he brought to me with just a touch was unreal. No mere human should be able to make me feel that good… But Sean was no mere human. He was a strong and smart and powerful alpha who loved me with everything he had.

"You starting without me?" Sean lifted the sheet off me and pinched my ass. "You know how hot that gets me."

I laughed and smacked at his thigh. "Whatever."

He yelped and hopped over me. "Oh, spanking. Now you're really speaking my language."

"How about you put that big alpha cock in my ass. That's my language."

He chuckled and kissed me hard on the mouth. "Whatever you want, sweetheart. Forever."